M000190937

AGAIN WITH YOU

MATCHBOX SERIES BOOK 4

EVEY LYON

Copyright © 2021 by EH Lyon

Again with You, Matchbox Series #4, First Edition

Written and published by: Evey Lyon

All rights reserved.

Editing & Formatting: Contagious Edits

Proofing: Katy Nielsen at Once Upon a Proofread

Cover Design: Kate Farlow. Y'All. That Graphic.

No part of this book may be reproduced in any form or by any electronic or mechanical means. Including information storage and retrieval systems, without written permission from the author, except for the use of brief quotations in a book review.

This book is a work of fiction. The names, characters, places, and incidents are products of the writer's imagination and used fictitiously and are not to be perceived as real. Any resemblance to persons, venues, events, businesses are entirely coincidental.

The author acknowledges the trademark status and trademark owners of various products referenced in this work of fiction, which have been used without permission. The publication/use of these trademarks is not authorized, associated with, or sponsored by the trademark owner.

E-book ISBN 978-1-7362792-3-6

Paperback ISBN 978-1-7362792-8-1

 Created with Vellum

MATCHBOX SERIES

Read the free & exclusive Series Prequel (short-story) here.

ABOUT

This sexy attorney may just have his second chance at a future with her...

Jake Sutton doesn't have time for romance. He tends to skip dinner and head straight to dessert. It's not like he's a complete jerk, he knows how to be romantic—it happened once. His friends have been trying to set him up on a blind date for months with the new bakery owner in town, to no avail. But when they end up at the same party and their eyes meet, it all comes back. Turns out Avery is no stranger.

Jake and Avery had a summer together a few years back in a different city. They were so many things... then one day they were not. Yet seeing each other again, well, it's a struggle—the not jumping into bed or lying her down on the kitchen counter kind of struggle.

But closure and a second chance are not the same thing, and they'll need both if they want to try again. And this bakery owner and hotshot attorney are about to realize that finding their way back to one another could just be bittersweet.

Again with You is the fourth sweet and sexy standalone novel from the "Matchbox" series, where you can revisit your favorite characters throughout.

CHAPTER ONE

JAKE

"Changes to clause 10.2 are not on the table. My client and I are losing patience and we have no problem walking. I am giving you until 9am on Monday to come back with a counteroffer worth negotiating," I bark into my phone before hanging up.

This week has been hectic to say the least. Finalized one deal only to walk into a shitstorm of another deal. Now, I am already late to casual drinks at Matchbox where my client/friend is planning to announce his surprise secret marriage—which gives this week a tint of crazy. Nobody knows they got hitched—except me, since I am the guy who arranged their marriage in a rush thanks to my connections.

Five years ago, I was living in Chicago on the verge of being named partner at a big-name firm with more than 80 billable hours per week. Now I have my own practice in Sage Creek, having something that *nearly* resembles a life outside of the office, and still billing a crazy amount of money per hour. Getting to watch deer walk down the idyllic main street of this Colorado town with a backdrop of mountains is just a bonus.

I focus on where I am, and Matchbox is happening tonight. An old warehouse now bar that has great live music, specialty drinks, and local brew. I'm about to grab the handle of the door, but my phone vibrates in my pocket again before I manage to succeed at opening the door.

Stepping back into the parking lot, I answer my phone as I pinch the bridge of my nose. "What do you want, Becca?" I tell my sister, and I can see my breath in the air as it is a freezing winter night.

She has a knack for catching me at the wrong moment.

"Fine, I will watch Stella for an *hour* Sunday, but really an *hour*. I have quite a lot to do this weekend... no, it's not work." *It is.* "Yeah, I saw Gramps... the doctors think he's doing okay... It's Gramps, of course he's stubborn... Okay... No, I am not interested in who you met at yoga. Listen, I gotta go, bye."

Great, I just got roped into watching my niece who can be a little terror, and my sister decided to remind me that Gramps, the greatest man alive, is in his final years. To top it off, she *still* tried to set me up with some random chick, because she feels I need to settle down.

Yeah, great way to end the week.

I head straight inside, and my eyes scan the joint. I head to the private area at the back where Leo and Lucas, my two friends, nod to me as I enter the room.

"You were a bulldozer this week. Owe you a big one for putting that negotiation to bed," Leo beams as his hand pats my shoulder. He is CEO of his family company that manages a lot of development deals, and he just so happens to have me on a high retainer fee to put out all his legal blazes.

"You can thank me when you get my bill," I remind him with a grin.

Lucas smiles as he gets up from his seat to welcome me. "It's been a few weeks, man. How have you been?"

Lucas and I went to graduate school together. He studied medicine and is now the local family doctor in town. We were close due to our equal desire to graduate and get the hell out of the Ivy League realm while still standing on solid ground.

"Yeah. Had a crazy few weeks in court, and Leo has been keeping me busy."

"Busy with work-work or secret weddings?" Lucas jokes as Leo just eloped.

Someone passes by with a tray of drinks and offers me the selection.

"Why do you think I grabbed a glass of champagne?" I give my best knowing grin.

Lucas nudges my arm. "You can finally meet Abby's cousin."

"Oh yeah, the new owner of Smokey Java's, right?"

Lucas has mentioned her once or twice, never got her name, though. Smokey Java's is a bakery next to Matchbox and always seems to be busy. But another person trying to get me on a blind date is the last thing I want right now.

By no means am I in a dry spell—okay, maybe recently, but I tend to skip the dating part and head straight into post-dinner activities.

I can be romantic—it happened once.

I just choose not to use that talent at this stage of my life. I am not a dick. In fact, most say I'm too sweet for my own good. I am just selective about when to use my gift of being a charming romantic guy who can make a woman scream with many O's.

While Leo is busy talking to his new wife, Jess, Lucas indicates his head to his girlfriend, Abby, who is sitting next to a woman... a beauty with blue eyes and light honey-brown hair to match her talented mouth. She is still wearing those dresses that don't deserve to be on her and could easily be ripped off, with those legs that wrap around my waist so I can take her deep—

What the fuck?

I *know* her.

My chest tightens and a sudden lack of oxygen hits me. Somebody could be yelling fire right now and I would have no clue, because everything just stopped.

This *has* to be the man upstairs playing a trick on me.

Lucas motions quietly. "That's Av—"

"Avery," I gulp out, my gaze unable to blink as I stare at her.

Lucas mumbles something, but I cannot distinguish what he is saying. I am too entranced by the sight in front of me. Avery has no clue that I am watching her as she tucks a few strands of loose hair behind her ear.

Just like that, there she is.

The one I could be romantic for, the one who I could be everything for.

The woman who changed my life, and then we parted ways like that summer needed to be put in a bottle, wrapped in chains to a brick of cement and sent to the bottom of the lake. Over time, I thought of her less often. But, truthfully, she still occupies my mind like a prime piece of real estate that will not sell.

My brain, body, and that muscle they call a heart are in a battle over what to do. In fact, that boot-camp training I was dragged to a few weeks ago did not prepare my heartrate for this.

I finish the champagne in my hand in one go as my eyes do not leave the scene in front of me.

Lucas gives me side-eye. "I know you're happy for Leo and Jess, but maybe go easy?" Lucas suggests with an entertained look as he steps closer to me.

I glance at him and my eyes must be blazing. "Yeah... a blast from the past," I say faintly, indicating my head to Avery in the corner talking with Abby.

"I gathered. What's the story?"

Looking into my empty glass, I say, "Remember I told you once about that relationship I had and how it was intense, life-changing—a mind-fuck, really?"

"Yeah." He gives me a nod.

I sigh. "It's her."

"What? Avery? Abby's cousin, Avery?" He too must repeat this news. "As in my live-in girlfriend's cousin who comes to family dinners and the new owner of Smokey Java's, Avery?" Lucas takes a beat and wipes a hand across his mouth. "Geez, I've been trying to set you two up on a blind date for months, but Avery said she doesn't date guys with the name Jake because she'd already done that once and it was enough."

Looking at him slightly, I am taken aback by that statement. Could it be that I am also still stuck in her head somewhere? How could I not be? We were...

Damn. We were so many things.

Lucas pats my back as he lets out a deep breath. "Oh man. This is complicated and crazy." He takes a sip of his beer.

"How have we not figured out this fact already?" I wonder aloud.

Lucas purses his lips. "Hmm, well, Avery is Abby's cousin from her mother's side, so different last names. Family photos in my house are reserved for my son and the dog that may as well be our child, so uh, I guess if you weren't really listening then you wouldn't have caught on. And Nate only calls Avery the cute bakery owner when he talks about her on our group runs."

My glare turns towards Lucas about the fact that his brother has in fact mentioned her on our runs, the cute bakery owner—who he'd better fucking stay away from.

Lucas scoffs. "You look like a man in warrior mode. Relax. Nate isn't interested." I feel not even slightly better.

"What is with this bar? Is there ever a normal night here?" I remark with disbelief, because really, anybody who walks into this place eventually comes out with a crazy story. Guess tonight it was my turn.

"But time changes people. Or maybe some people need a long pause before facing each other," Lucas offers the unsolicited advice, because he and Abby came together only recently, after knowing one another their whole lives. He sometimes presents life as a freaking fairytale.

There is nothing more than wanting to believe he is right. I have thought about it every day for the past five years.

Five freaking years.

And look at her. Still beautiful. Is she faintly smiling? Please no, it's too infectious. That dress? So easy to slide up her...

Letting out an exhale, something snaps in me.

This woman left a mark on my life and no way am I letting her escape again without a fight. No, this is the woman that sent my world into a tailspin, and something tells me we are not done on that ride. I've been waiting for this chance, and I wasn't even looking. I should have been searching.

I look to Lucas and give him a devilish grin. "Can you introduce us?"

He knows I have plans on my mind.

"You two already know each other," Lucas states, amused, as he crosses his arms.

"Yeah, but I want to meet her again."

CHAPTER TWO

"THIS TASTES SO GOOD, AVERY!" ABBY, MY COUSIN, beams as she comes and sits next to me on the low oversized leather love seat. She tucks into a piece of simple chocolate cake on her small plate.

Our friends literally just casually announced they're married as they passed around glasses of champagne.

"What can I say? I take my party responsibilities seriously," I joke, clucking the side of my cheek with my tongue. Because I baked the wedding cake Jess had asked me to make and swore me to secrecy as I own Smokey Java's, the social-media worthy, travel-blog hyped, ridiculously named bakery/café next to Matchbox. Rumor has it we may even be nominated for a local award.

After working in the corporate world, I decided to take my chances and follow my hobby. It's only been a few months into it, but I feel confident with my choice. Taste testing new treats may be killing me, but I am doing my best to balance it with green smoothies and afternoon runs.

Which is also why I feel confident in my dark blue V-neck dress that shows a little triangle of skin in the front. It is casual, yet cute. I grab my glass of champagne and take a sip of the bubbly liquid, listening vaguely to our friend Harper—who has a wedding of her own coming up—talk about wedding ideas from Pinterest, which in her world is clearly the place that holds the answers to all humanity.

Looking around, I see great people, but they are also all soaking in their happily ever after. Max and Harper met when she was his client, buying real estate through his company. Abby and Lucas were united after they both went through divorces with other people. Jess and Leo just pulled off a secret wedding. It's not that I'm moping around as everyone lives in their bliss, because I most certainly am not. This mid-height beauty knows her time will come.

It's just... it's been so long.

"Jake is coming, right?" Lucas asks Leo loud enough for my ears to perk up.

Here we go again, because Lucas has mentioned this Jake guy a few times as a potential date for me. But I was once with a Jake when I lived in Chicago, and to be honest, there is only one in my book.

Been there, done that, and wore his t-shirt kind of situation.

By default, Lucas's friend has no chance as I would never get past the name. So, I never bothered to hear the whole pitch for why I should go on a date with the guy.

"Yeah, he should be stopping by any moment now for a round," Leo confirms. "He was busy finalizing the legalities of a deal for me like the shark he is. Owe the guy a bottle of Matchbox's finest," he says, then quickly looks back to his new wife who is sitting on his lap.

Out of the corner of my eye, I notice Lucas grin as he gets up from his seat to welcome the new arrival to the room. "It's been a few weeks, man. How have you been?" I hear.

"Yeah. Had a crazy case load and Leo has been keeping me busy," that voice explains a little cheekily.

It sends a chill down my spine. It is too familiar. Way *too* familiar.

I know it. I remember it.

Wait a sec...

The name Jake, plus Leo mentioned legalities. That equates to law. Which means it could be assumed this Jake guy is a lawyer or attorney.

Holy mother of... What are the chances that the guy whose t-shirt I wore after screaming his name many times... is their Jake? The mathematical odds of this surely are not high.

"Busy with work-work or secret weddings?" Lucas jokes.

That voice laughs. *That* vibrant laugh. "Why do you think I grabbed a glass of champagne?" he answers.

I already know the smirk slapped across his face as he says it. It is a mix of charisma and trouble, yet so incredibly warm. Maybe a dimple appears too.

My mind has an overflow of memories, I get utterly lost in thought. I continue to listen to my cousin speak and throw on a faint smile as I pretend to listen; I have no idea what she's even saying. No concept of time either, as a rushing feeling of blood flows to my chest. I'm only brought back to reality when I hear someone say my name.

"I guess you haven't met Avery yet. Let me introduce you two," Lucas announces.

I do not want my eyes to look up. I do not want the confirmation that the voice is the voice I remember.

The one that charmed me, melted me, comforted me,

and then became too painful to be around, yet I still dream of.

My body tenses and everything sinks to the pit of my stomach. Pretty sure my heart is racing on the scale of a rocket going to Mars. Taking a deep breath, I do what any confident woman would do.

Slowly tipping my head up as I am sitting, and he is standing over me like an incredible hulk in a fine-cut expensive suit.

Because I *know* he is in a suit.

This is not happening....

But. It. Is.

Our eyes meet like lightning striking. But really, this situation has the forecast of an incoming hurricane. Those same brown eyes. *His* brown eyes.

We need no introduction.

"It's been a long time, Ave," he greets me with a soft low voice that has a mix of surprise thrown in. Yet his face tells me he enjoys my shock.

I look at him and he appears more filled-in across the arms and broad shoulders—has he been working out? But for the most part, he is still the same. Suit, chocolate-brown hair perfectly cut, brown eyes, and square jaw with a five o'clock shadow. Perfect height, slender body, strong arms, chiseled chest, sculpted back...

My brain has a quick overload of every inch of him that was memorized and stored in the back of my head.

My jaw must be dropping as my eyes join his for a different type of hello, one that nobody in the room would notice, but for us it is far too familiar.

"This has to be a dream," I mutter softly to myself.

"So, I *am* still in your dreams?" His clever grin confirms that I was not quiet enough.

"I guess you two know each other?" Lucas wonders as he looks between us oddly. But his face tells me he is playing along.

Why, yes. Yes, we do. Your Jake is my Jake.

This is a small world.

"Jake," I let it finally escape my mouth.

There is a pause, but I realize Lucas is looking at us all too curiously.

"Yeah, uhm, Jake is a friend of my brother's, actually," I try to explain while swallowing the lump in my throat and looking away from Jake's gaze.

That gaze that did things to me then and it seems to do things to me now too, because a wave of heat just went through me and is coiling at the internal walls of my center.

A friend of my brother's is true. But that is not all he is.

We were a wildfire together, and then the universe gave us a sign that we should let the blaze burn, leaving us in ashes.

"Yeah, right, a friend of your brother's," he echoes and gives me a neutral look. "It's been what, five years?" His gaze pierces me with a superpower that scientists have yet to discover.

"I will be right back. Forgot to get something for the cake," I explain with a thrown-on closed-lip smile, and high-tail it towards the general bar where it is busy and buzzing.

I grab the bar with my hands as I have a mini internal meltdown and try to breathe deep breaths, indicating to Nate for a whiskey. My cousin Abby once tried to set me up on a date with the bar's owner, Lucas's brother, Nate. But a rugged ex-hockey player is not really my type.

No. My type are guys who seem to get better with age and who reappear five years later.

I need something strong for this.

I can face him. I need to do this.

Those eyes—oh God—those warm brown eyes. Something in me still aches from the last day I saw him, and equally something floats in my chest with possibility.

Possibility? Why would I think that?

Really need that drink now.

Abby finds me and touches my back softly.

"So, you know Jake Sutton?" Abby gently states more than asks, as she tucks her light brown hair to the side.

I nod yes as I focus my gaze forward to watch Nate prepare my glass of whiskey like it is the challenge of the century.

"How do you know him?" I ask, trying to put these puzzle pieces together of how he is here.

"He went to graduate school with Lucas, and they're friends. Jake also does some legal work for Leo and they're friends. He doesn't come that often to our friend dinners and brunches, but he does stop by occasionally. So, in case you haven't gathered, he is everyone's friend, and you will continue to collide with him at social gatherings," she informs me with a weak smile.

"How do *you* know him?" she adds.

"He was a friend of Greg's. They went to university—I mean, undergrad together," I grab my glass of whiskey and drink it for dear life.

"And something more?" Abby enquires, tenderly touching my shoulder, again hinting that I can't fool her.

I give her a slight nod in confirmation.

"A lot more," I exhale.

I would tell her everything, but now is not the time. Abby is smart and picks up that this conversation requires a different setting, and she'll no doubt ask about it again later.

"How is it possible that I haven't run into him yet?" I

wonder. Sage Creek is not that big, but a just-big-enough town in Colorado that tourists flock to and where locals live in bliss. Everyone knows everyone. So how we missed this detail of living so close is a fact I cannot process.

Abby shrugs. "I mean, he wasn't at Lucas's birthday party because he had that birthday party for his niece."

"And I wasn't at your holiday party as I visited my brother." Abby and I are listing all the times that would have made sense for me and Jake to cross paths, but we clearly didn't. "Guess we were bound to run into one another eventually, and tonight is that night."

She gives me a loving smile that only relatives can give and then heads back towards the group.

Taking another gulp of whiskey, I let the burn hit my throat. My face must be crooked from the aggressive gulp I just swallowed. After debating, I decide I should probably head back and face the music. But as I turn away from the bar, I do not get far.

Jake—who must have casually undone the top two buttons of his sexy shirt—is slowing his pace as he approaches me.

Our eyes meet for an intense standoff.

They darken.

"So, you need something strong too?" He tries to break the ice gently.

Because this guy knows how to ease us into situations. Now, he is standing within touching distance of me and stealing my air.

"Ave, I had no idea that you would be here."

I look away because my head has not decided yet how I should feel. "This is definitely a surprise," I manage to say as I try to avoid his gaze.

"Yeah, you made sure of that when you let five years get

between us," he replies directly with resentment in his voice.

My eyes flick up to him because I am a little taken aback by his abruptness. But at the same time, I deserve it.

He pinches the bridge of his nose and lets out a deep sigh. "Sorry, I didn't mean for it to come out like that," he apologizes and continues, "but what are you doing *here*?" he asks, slightly shaking his head as if he needs to double-check that I am still in front of him.

The bonus question of the night, clearly.

My eyes cannot stop looking at the man in front of me. He was *my* man; we were supposed to be bound together forever.

I realize that I need to answer him.

"Moved here in the summer. I'm the new owner of Smokey Java's, actually," I explain and let my mouth take another decent swig of whiskey, so much so that the glass is empty.

His lips curve slightly up. "You finally moved away from the advertising agency?" he says, intrigued, familiar with my past and maybe happy that something for me worked out.

I nod barely.

"...And you finally got your own practice, I take it?" I can't help but show I am happy for him, with my mouth forming a smile.

He nods at me with the same look. "I moved from Chicago about three years ago. My parents live an hour away. Still, how did we not cross paths yet?" We both look at each other, realizing our lives have changed. Yet, something stays in the air between us. A familiar ease floats between us like time has not passed.

There is a pause, but in that pause, I realize that this is

the guy that once made my heart skip, my skin crawl, and my body melt. And all he had to do was give me that smile.

But that was five years ago. Time brings change, people change. He could probably have a wife at home with 2.5 kids and a dog. Like he deserves. He is just trying to be polite and catch up.

But wait, he does *not* have that hypothetical family. I know this because Lucas tried to set Jake and me up once. Something in me races, and it's the kind of race that floods you with adrenaline. Enough adrenaline to help the whiskey give me that liquid courage I need to look into his eyes.

And I do.

"This is kind of crazy, right?" My words drag out as my eyelashes flutter and my eyes meet his. Maybe my face softens and my mouth slants slightly upwards too.

His face cracks the same look too as he rubs his strong hand across his jaw and leans against the bar. *Those hands...*

"It is. But running into each other randomly at a bar is not new for us. It happened once before." He studies me then cocks his head slightly to the side. "Want another drink?"

With him?

One day, but not tonight.

A drink with him requires a trip down memory lane, and even the upcoming tequila shots our group have planned cannot prepare me for that trip. I need time to adjust to the fact that this guy is living within a five-mile radius of me.

"Really, I think we should head back in there. Someone mentioned something about a toast for the newlyweds or something." I ignore his attempt to dive into deep conversation.

He steps away from the bar and closer to me. Touching my arm as someone walks by to reach the bar. It makes me catch my breath. He must feel that electric wave that just passed through me, because truthfully, this man knows my body more than anyone. Those fingers are still dominating and leading, I can feel it with only his fingertips on my skin.

"I didn't think I would see you again," I admit out of nowhere with my eyes peering up to his. There is pain in my voice, that I am sure of.

"I know the feeling."

Jake lets his fingers graze up my arm. I'm in a short-sleeved dress, which means his fingertips caress my bare skin, making my body shiver gently and my nipples form taut buds.

"Maybe we could have a whiskey together?" he asks again tenderly. His fingers have not stopped touching me and he stares at his fingers as if he is remembering how they once explored my every inch.

My lips tug up in response. "You are still persistent."

"It's you, Ave. I am not going to see you and then ignore you for the night. We could probably both use another drink. I mean, how the hell am I supposed to sleep tonight?"

With me. Whoa, where did that thought come from? Filter it, Avery.

"I'm asking myself the same question, but I think tonight isn't the night for a reunion."

His fingers drop from my arm and already I want them back.

A scoff escapes his mouth. "Reunion? Sure, if that's what we want to call it." He looks away from me, but then lets his head lazily spin back to my direction. "We need to talk." It rolls out of his mouth.

I turn my head away in slight sadness, but dammit, I know he's right.

"Are you free this weekend? For a coffee? Maybe we can talk a little?" he asks—no, he pleads innocently.

My body is in flee mode. Because a talk? That would be the right thing to do. What we need to do. But that realization alone is making me need to remind myself to breathe.

"This really is a surprise, and I am not sure how long my head will need before it stops spinning," I respond simply, because as much as it is the right thing to do, to talk...

The jury is still out on if I am strong enough to.

CHAPTER THREE

JAKE: 5 YEARS AGO

My thumb scrolls through my work e-mails on my phone in one hand, and there's a clean scotch firm in my other. I'm waiting at the bar in the upscale lounge where my colleagues normally go for a drink after work. The place has smooth dark oak yet modern furniture, and is the choice of many who work off Michigan Avenue in the Near North Side in Chicago.

"You really crushed them in there. I'm sure by this time next year you'll be a named partner," Chris, my colleague tells me as he finishes his whiskey.

I shrug it off, "Maybe."

"Shit, I wish I had your balls. You bill too many hours, which means you work all weekend, and it seems by the wandering eyes around this place that you can take home whomever you want," Chris admires.

A laugh escapes me. "Hey, man, you're doing great. Your work on that deposition helped get us to where we needed to be today. Plus, you have a newborn, so I would certainly hope that you're not working on the weekends." I do my best to encourage him as my eyes roam the room.

"Want another drink, Chris?" I ask, and he nods.

Just then a woman cuts in front of me to speak to the bartender. She mumbles excuse me and I must do a double-take. She seems familiar. My brain does a flip through the catalogue of women stored in my head. It quickly figures it out as she does a double-take too.

"Don't I know you?" I ask with an amused grin.

She looks at me, lets her brain catch up, and smiles. "Jake, right?"

"Yeah. And you are Greg's little sister, Avery."

"Small world," she remarks with slight disbelief.

Greg Lewis is an old buddy from college. During college we hung out, but since then, I only hear from him on an occasional basis. Last time I saw Avery she was at a party at Greg's frat house. Why Greg thought bringing a barely-18-year-old girl looking like Avery was a good idea was beyond me. Avery was every guy's fantasy and barely legal then, and something told me she was not as innocent as her brother thought.

Geez, I'm getting old, because I am pushing towards the big 3-0, which makes Avery what, 24 now is my guess?

"Your brother would kill me if I didn't get you a drink and ask how you are. Want one?" I ask, giving her my best look.

She seems to be letting her eyes assess me. "I was going to go actually, but why not?"

Chris nudges me. "Sorry, man, I need to head out. The missus isn't having a great night with the baby."

"Good luck with that," I tell him, but my eyes don't leave Avery. In no time, he's gone, and I think I may be happy about that.

Her blue eyes find me with her sweet-looking lips giving me a smile. Christ, she is a sight for sore eyes.

And *very* legal now.

"So, long time." She's rather chirpy as she takes her short black jacket off and throws it on the back of the barstool. Her fitted blue dress and black heels attached to her smooth and toned legs tell me she probably just came from work.

"Yeah, a long time indeed. How are you?" I give her a reassuring smile and a quick side hug before she sits down. Ooh, she smells good. "What are you having?" I ask, sitting back down and indicating to the bartender to come and take her order. She asks for the same as me as if it's her usual.

"You're a scotch drinker?" I crack out, skeptical. Her grin with her pink lip gloss is sexier than it should be.

She nods yes like I asked a crazy question. "Actually, mezcal is my favorite lately, but that seems a little too festive for a casual Friday-night drink," she smiles.

"I guess you're no longer a kid anymore," I comment, taking a sip from my glass as my lips quirk.

"For someone who knows the law, you missed the detail that I was very legal when I saw you last time." Her head cocks a little to the right and her words roll playfully off her tongue. Maybe even dirtier than it should.

Keep this professional, man, a favor for an old buddy.

"You're in town for work or did you move here? I guess last time I saw you, you were deciding on which college to attend," I ask as I grab my phone and shoot out a text to Greg that I ran into his sister.

"Yeah. That is true. It was a Halloween party when I last saw you, right? You left early to be a good student, I guess," she reminisces. "Greg mentioned once you did extremely well with your LSATS then headed off to Yale for graduate school, so I guess it makes sense why parties weren't your thing."

I hold a hand up. "Whoa, parties were my thing in college, you just caught me on an off day," I protest with a slight grin and adjust my neck.

"Fair enough. You met my brother in a library, though, right?" she counters with a coy look.

"True. But if it is any consolation, I was on the lacrosse team in high school and not always into studying," I joke.

She squeezes my arm playfully. "Ooh, a lacrosse player? Well, isn't that crazy and wild," she retorts with sarcasm.

I shake my head at her banter. "But enough about me. What did you end up studying?"

She takes a sip of her scotch and pushes her glass in front of her. "I studied business, and to answer your original question, I am on a project here for the summer. I work for an advertising agency specializing in clients from the food and beverage industry. You're a lawyer, right? Please tell me not a divorce lawyer or something boring like that." A smile forms at the corner of her mouth and she seems genuinely interested.

I like her energy.

"Yeah, an attorney, actually, and made it to the dark side of corporate law. So, no divorces for me." I scratch my jaw.

Her hand touches my arm, and it ignites a slight zing in my body. "Well then, if I get arrested for public indecency, I know which lawyer not to call," she jokes, and it makes me crack a grin. "I guess corporate law is a lot of mergers and acquisitions."

The way that spins off her tongue and the way her eyebrows move tell me her mind is definitely *not* innocent. Move swiftly on from that, Jake. *Just do it.*

"Four months here is not exactly a short time. Your boyfriend must not like that."

Why did I just throw that in?

She lets out a laugh. "No boyfriend, so not an issue." Her eyes assess me. "Your girlfriend enjoys that you spend more time at the office than on her?" she blurts out with ease.

Immediately, I choke on my drink and clear my throat.

Whoa. The flow of energy moves strong with this one.

"No girlfriend, so not an issue," I manage to crack out and lock my eyes on her. Studying her, she seems very pleased with my answer.

What the hell is happening here? But I am enjoying this, *a lot.*

My phone pings, and it's a text from Greg.

Crazy! I was going to text you that she's in town and ask if you could check up on her. We should catch up soon, it's been a while, man.

I show the message to Avery.

She grabs her scotch glass and holds it out to me. "So, I guess you're checking up on me for my brother."

I nod as we clink our glasses. I notice the way she swallows the scotch and the movement of her throat, thinking things that her brother most definitely would *not* approve of.

"Greg would probably want me to call him and give the full report, but I'm happy to meet up with a familiar face too." It's genuine because a break from work is sometimes invigorating. She nods once slowly, doubting my tone.

"You enjoy marketing?"

"Truthfully, it isn't what it's cracked up to be. Everything is now about social media. Plus, living in San Francisco just aggravates that social-media life. A bit too pretentious for me, and it gets exhausting. In a fairy tale, I would own a bakery or something," she shrugs.

Her thumb rubs her lower lip, and it leaves me to wonder what else her mouth could do.

"Why don't you?"

"That would most definitely ruin my parents' plans of me finding a husband, becoming a stay-at-home mom, and wasting my degree they paid for. I mean, you know Greg. He went into medicine, and although he's a good doctor, I always wonder if he would have preferred law. But Dad wanted him to practice medicine." She is brutally honest and sounds like she doesn't have a problem saying it how it is, nor does she plan on following her parents' roadmap.

It's refreshing.

"But," she challenges, "you can't honestly tell me you also want to be working the rest of your life in the city for some large law firm that counts your hours?"

I look at her for a moment.

She's not too shy to ask what is on her mind. I'm not used to that. I'm used to having a drink with women just to be polite, so we keep conversation simple and quick before leaving to do other things. Avery is authentic, she's not asking just to make conversation. She wants to know truthfully. It is what I sense from her, at least.

I shrug a shoulder. "Maybe you're right. I don't want to stay forever in a big firm. Maybe have my own practice. But a private practice is easier done in a small town, I guess. Maybe I would move closer to my family in Colorado one day. My sister Becca just had a baby, so she begs me to move all the time. But I'm doing too well here to give it up," I reflect, not sure I've actually ever said that aloud.

A warm smile spreads across her face. "See? Sounds like you also have other plans for another chapter, and I hope you get it. Sounds idyllic." That sentence floats around in the air.

It makes me smile to myself.

She plays with her long hair, bringing it up into a ponytail but then letting it fall back down. My guess is it's a natural move for her, but I've already been drawn in to where I could attack the meeting point between her neck and ear.

"You're not originally from Chicago, right?" she enquires.

"Actually, I am. Kind of. Well, the north-west suburbs. But most of my family moved to Colorado when my dad's job transferred him there when I was in college. Are you always based in San Francisco since Chicago is only a project?"

"Since I graduated, yeah. That was two years ago. I'm hoping to move if I get a promotion at the end of the summer. Funny, I also have family in Colorado, and I try to get out there during ski season."

A small break in our conversation happens and she picks up on this.

"Maybe you can help me with your local knowledge. Do you have any recommendations for bakeries around here? I want to try a few this weekend." She swirls on her bar stool, back and forth.

"Yeah, there are a few. I can send you a list. Do you have a lot of plans for the weekend?"

Why am I asking?

"No, maybe some work, a yoga class, and hopefully some decent pieces of carrot cake."

A guy comes to the bar and reaches over her to pay for his drinks. My arm finds its way around Avery's upper back and shoulder to move her out of the way, moving her towards me gently, and her eyes shoot up to look at me. Her eyes are big and sparkly.

My arm stays protective around her a few seconds longer than needed, and I may just have caught a glimpse of her black bra strap. My lips tug a little bit, but not enough to give her a full smile as my eyes give her a gleam.

When she gives me a look of gratitude, I let her go. But my arm would sure as hell have been happy if it could have stayed put.

Quickly moving us on.

"Carrot cake is a good choice. Chocolate is too predictable, and vanilla is just pure sugar." I give her my best warm smile and she returns a similar look.

"Actually, I love making carrot cake, so I'm always searching for new recipes."

"Homemade carrot cake is impressive. Feel free to drop off a piece if you bake one while you're in town." That sounded polite with zero other intentions, I think.

She seems satisfied with my sentence and gives me a look that is far more seductive than she likely means for it to be. My decency scale is about to break.

"I will, but then I'll need to know where you live." She's coy. Her eyebrows arch like she's playing a game.

I take a big gulp of scotch that leaves my glass empty, my cue to get the hell out of here.

But it's Friday and that means I have no reason not to have a good night. Our rhythm of conversation is fast moving, and we are already at a point where I sense this isn't just friendly chit chat. Avery knows how to send off vibes, and something tells me she is not innocently giving signals.

Okay, just be a man. A smart man who has passed the state bar. Cross-examine the hell out of this girl, because I am certain her mind is somewhere it should not be. But I certainly hope it to be.

Her fingers tap her empty glass.

"Want another scotch?" I ask because I am a gentleman.

"Nope." It comes out simple.

"Want to get out of here?"

"Yes." Her eyes fly up to meet mine with her lips parting.

"Where do you want to go?" I look directly in her eyes, giving her a warning.

"Do you always cross-examine?" she retorts as if she has known me for years.

We are familiar with each other, but not enough for her to know that was *exactly* what I was doing.

Her hand touches my arm, which is a nice feeling, by the way. I let my head shake side to side in amusement. Avery knows the game, and I have about 30 seconds to decide if this is a road I want to go down.

"Want to have a drink at my place?"

She nods yes, with her eyes giving me an agreeable, almost worshiping look, her mouth curving slightly up.

I have a lot of plans for her, but truthfully, they don't involve a drink.

"You don't want a drink, do you?" I tell her more than I ask.

Her free hand lets her fingers walk up my chest and her eyes angle up to meet mine. "No. No, I don't." She sounds sultry and determined.

A sound escapes from the back of my throat, satisfied, and I throw some money on the bar and guide her out with my hand firmly placed on her lower back.

The moment the door opens to my condo, she turns to me and walks backwards slowly. Taking off her jacket and letting it fall to the floor. She turns around, and I step behind her to unzip her dress slowly as she pulls her hair to the side. Her head slightly turns back to me with her mouth parted and eyes inviting me in.

Avery turns around again and lets her dress fall to the floor, so she is left in black heels with matching black panties and bra that seem to be smooth and silky.

Throwing my suit jacket to the floor, I undo the cuff of my sleeves as I follow her towards my bedroom as if she knows the floorplan by heart.

Watching her. Craving her.

Her look and her sway draw me in.

Avery's fingers reach for my shirt and give me a tug towards her. She finds my buttons and slowly loosens each one as if she's a professional at doing this, our eyes not parting, the anticipation growing. Pressure building in my groin. Her smell of vanilla keeping me aware of what we are doing.

I step closer to her. I'm done for, as she is a mixture of sugar and spice and everything nice. She is fucking hot, to put it in plain terms.

The moment comes where we kick it up a notch. I back her into the hallway wall heading towards my bedroom, away from the living room that is open with floor-to-ceiling windows overlooking the city. Only the light from the night city coming through the windows and the small light by the front door offer us enough to see clearly what we're doing.

Her eyes bounce back and forth between my eyes and my lips until she focuses only on my mouth. I let out a slight warning laugh from the back of my throat, almost a growl. Wrapping my arm around her waist, pulling her to me, she lets out a surprised moan from what I can guess is the feeling of my throbbing cock pushing against her stomach. With no hesitation, I push her against the wall, and I dive my lips onto hers. Our mouths collide with each other, my mouth taking ownership of her and finding her tongue, which seems to be welcoming me with equal force.

It is feverish, hard, and raw. She tastes like a mixture of scotch and strawberry. Devilish.

Somehow, I knew with that kiss that she was going to leave a mark on my life.

CHAPTER FOUR

It was calculated. I left my umbrella at Jake's place after getting a taxi before he woke.

This is not the start of a relationship. This is sex.

I am not the type to sleep with strangers. He is not a stranger.

Nor do I sleep around.

It has been a while since I felt I had an opportunity like that, and I knew when I saw him sitting there in that three-piece suit that him doing things to me was a fantasy I should initiate.

When I first agreed to let Jake buy me a drink, I didn't think much about it. It was just an old friend of my brother's whom I had met a few times and vaguely remembered as good-looking and probably skilled in *many* things.

While he ordered a round of drinks, I Googled his name, and the charmer does not do social media, which left me to resort to searching his profile on his law firm's site. Although I felt a little stalkerish for a millisecond, it was enough to tip me over the edge of interest, and I was happy I stayed for a drink.

I gave him my calm and confident approach. And he played the game like a pro. His ability to make me come was also award-worthy... twice.

But I am only in town for a short while, so I'm not looking for a boyfriend. By the look of his dining table filled with work, something tells me he does not have much space in his life for anything else.

Yet, I left my umbrella.

My eyes look up at Jake as he enters the trendy café in the Near North Side of the city, not far from the lake. The place tries to live up to its reviews as being hip, with framed Nirvana and Rolling Stones posters. And the two ladies behind me talking about a blind date gone wrong tells me this place is half-decent with its clientele.

Jake gives me a sly smirk as he slowly walks towards me like an animal approaching its prey. And I will gladly be his prey again.

It may be the weekend, but he does not seem to retire the button-down shirts, as demonstrated by his light blue shirt paired with jeans.

He slides the umbrella onto the table. "I think you forgot something." Sitting down across from me, his grin is charming. "You are something, huh?" he remarks and then indicates to the waiter for a coffee as he sets his sunglasses on the table with his phone.

I rest my head on my hand, my propped elbow on the table. "Why, whatever do you mean?" I pretend to be confused, little theatrics thrown in for good measure.

"Taking off before the sheets are even cold is a bold move." His head tilts to the side.

"Nah. It's easier that way," I say confidently, sipping from my mug of coffee.

He brushes it off. "So, did you speak to your brother?"

"Yeah. I said it was nice meeting up with you, but you seem quite busy so don't think I will see you again. But something tells me you don't really care about his opinion." My head tilts at an angle with my eyes scanning him.

He scratches his head. "No, I don't. Greg is an old buddy from college, but I do not consider him close enough that his little sister is off limits. *Obviously*." Jake is confident, borderline cocky.

And I like it.

"What limits would those be?" I dare him.

He rubs his face. "What world did you come from?" he asks in amazement, trying to hide his grin, and I have to smile.

I decide to level with him and cross my arms on the table, my voice nearing low as I lean in. "Thanks for last night, by the way. It was a good time."

Sinking into his chair, his lips curve in as he tries not to let that grin swipe across his face. "Anytime."

My eyebrow arches and my head cocks in curiosity. "Anytime?"

He clears his throat as he pushes his sleeves up and leans into the table. "Yeah. Why not?"

Biting my tongue, I study him. "True. I need to focus on this project, and I am gone in September and you are obviously a workaholic, so why not have a little fun?" I look away to see who's in the café and also to avoid his smoldering gaze that may just make me blush and give me a need to cross my legs.

"Workaholic?" He gives me a bewildered look.

I let out a laugh. "Please don't pretend. Last night you were most likely skimming your work e-mails instead of checking the score of the Cubs game while you waited for your colleague."

He purses his lips in amusement. "True, but it pays off in my professional career."

"Modest." I manage to say it straight-faced, but truthfully, he was a little arrogant there.

Jake studies me up and down. Resting his arms on the table, he looks at me. "And for the record, I do have fun," he clarifies. "But tell me why you were so determined last night at the bar."

An exhale escapes me, and I debate how honest to be. But I understand why clients flock to him for his legal skills. It's his personality. He has the ability to make you open up to him like a book on display, and all he has to do is smile.

"Can this be attorney-client confidentiality or—?"

"You're not my client, but this can be we've-screwed-in-my-bed confidentiality." He gives me a humorous look.

"Fine. I would love to say I've been harboring a crush since I was 18, but truthfully, I didn't wait six years for you," I deadpan to ensure he does not let his ego inflate. "I know you, trust you, and something told me you are experienced and know exactly what you're doing. And you proved that theory right." It comes out firm and I think effective as the corner of his mouth moves.

He taps his fingers on the table. "Fair enough."

He studies me, his tongue gliding along his teeth, and I wonder if he picks up on the fact that I may just be asking him to rock my world, send me to oblivion, find new galaxies, etc.

"So, let me guess, you left your umbrella on purpose to see if maybe we can replay last night." He insinuates the fact while licking his lips with a grin forming.

I slant my shoulders and try not to crack a smile.

"And you returned it. So here we are again." I let my

forehead furrow. A deep laugh comes out from his mouth that knows how to devour.

He leans in closer to the table. "You know, I actually have a bottle of mezcal in my fridge."

Ah, he remembers my love for the drink.

My cheeks tighten as I try to keep my delight in. "Is that an observation or an invitation?"

"Having fun sounds good, and consider it an invitation." He is smooth and enticing as he says it, with his lips twitching as if his mind already has plans for me.

My fingers draw vague circles on the table as I look at him with soft eyes. "Invitation accepted." It comes out with more smolder than I intended, but my want cannot seem to hide.

"But, Avery, no more running off while the sheets are still warm. We are not in a relationship, but this is Chicago. I don't like the idea of you heading off alone in the dark, even if it is in a cab." His eyes do not leave me, and he is firm. But it comes out caring, protective, and it makes something in me flutter.

"You must have a lot of women who've slept in your bed then."

"No. I only have this rule with you." He seems dead serious.

I study him for a second, and I should ask him more, but I decide to let it go and I nod in understanding.

The waitress returns with his coffee.

"Actually, can you make this to-go? Also, a piece of carrot cake too. This should cover us." He hands the waitress cash, far more than needed.

That is kind of sweet he remembers my carrot cake.

In 20 minutes flat, we are back at his place, and the moment his front door closes he pushes me against the wall, and we go at it like animals... Clothes being yanked, hands pushing, mouths pulling, teeth biting, lips kissing, as my legs wrap around his waist.

I pull away, breathless, my lips swollen. "Guess we are skipping the mezcal," I tease, and he looks at me with a devilish grin.

Setting me down, he takes my hand and guides me to the kitchen. We are only in our underwear and my black bra somehow managed to stay on.

He opens the fridge and grabs a very expensive bottle of mezcal before taking a glass from the cupboard.

"Only one glass?" I ask as I hop on the counter.

He gives me a seductive look. "We can share." His eyes do not leave me as he pours a glass with haste, some of the liquid spilling over the edges. Jake takes a decent sip and then brings the glass to my mouth. My eyes give him a knowing look as I slowly take a sip of the bitter-tasting liquid.

"I have a better idea," I whisper. Taking the glass, my finger dips into the cold liquid, and then I use my finger to rub the drink on his inner wrist near his watch. Making sure he is looking at me, my eyes observe him as my tongue licks his inner pulse. His face tells me he is pleased, to which I respond by placing a soft kiss on the very same spot.

"Your mind and my mind have a lot in common." He grins as he takes the bottle and pours a little on my neck that arches back, and I laugh. When his tongue finds my bare neck, my arms loop around him as his mouth moves to caress my bare shoulder.

A soft gentle moan escapes me. "Since our minds have so much in common, then you know what I'm thinking?" I smile as I lean back to lie down on the counter.

His sexy look gives me a warning as he pours a little

from the bottle onto my bare stomach near my naval. When he sets the bottle down and his warm mouth breathes close to my stomach, he pulls my hips to the edge of the counter with his eyes blazing up at me. His fingers find the edge of my panties; I know that this man knows exactly what I am thinking.

We do not make it to the bed. Not that round, anyhow.

But when we finally decide to take a break after two rounds, I am lying in his bed with the sheet entangled around me, my hair a wild mess. The way he looks at me tells me he is enjoying the view.

"Do you want a t-shirt or something?" he asks, emerging from the bathroom after disposing of the condom.

"Oh yeah, you have that *no rushing off when the sheets are warm* rule. Sure."

He tosses me an old Chicago Bears shirt that I throw on.

"Was I a little rough?" he asks with an innocent smile as he pulls on a new t-shirt.

"The claw marks on your shoulder tell me I can take it just fine," I respond, letting my knees move side to side as I lie there lazily.

He studies me for what feels like a good minute as he leans against the dresser with his arms crossed. "Not sure why I gave you a shirt. It's only going to come off during the night."

I let out an enjoyable laugh as he comes and flops on the bed, lying next to me on his side, looking at me, his fingers caressing my arm that I am leaning my weight against.

The way he looks at me tells me he has something to say, and his voice is soft. "I'm really busy. I bill almost 80 hours some weeks. But you should stop by when you can while you're in town."

And with his eyes having a glint, I know what he means.

My bottom lip is stuck between my teeth, and then I let out a sigh. "We are two smart people. This is just fun. And we do have fun. I also need to focus on this project at work." I study him for a clue of how I should answer. His eyes are locked on me with anticipation. "But I might be able to make an exception here or there when my work allows."

His soft nod tells me he is satisfied. "Settled."

An inviting smile emerges on my mouth. "Any other requests?"

His smile is flirtatious, and his other hand comes to cup the back of my neck as he brings my head closer to him so he can whisper in my ear. "I have a whole list," he warns in a deep low voice, and it makes me grin.

I get comfortable on the pillow as he leans to the edge to look at his watch on the side table. I noticed it before. It's classic with a brown band and silver face.

"What's the story with the watch?"

Jake leans back in the bed and puts his arms behind his head.

"My grandfather's. He gave it to me when I passed the bar to practice law," he recalls.

"You're close with him?"

"Yeah. We would always play checkers on Wednesdays, but we moved him out to Colorado to be closer to my parents after my grandma passed. He is still pretty healthy, stubborn as a goat, and chases the nurses like he's still a teenager. But it is easier that way—being closer to my parents, I mean."

"Sounds like he's a cool guy."

Maybe I feel I need to comfort him with that fact. For some reason, I grab his left wrist where he normally wears his watch and I place a soft gentle kiss on his inner pulse point. He doesn't seem to mind.

Without thought, we find our way into each other's arms. We don't question it. But this seems like we are already dangerously crossing lines.

Maybe so, yet neither of us have the sense to complain.

CHAPTER FIVE

JAKE

I HAVE BEEN TO SMOKEY JAVA'S MANY TIMES. JUST NOT recently.

The place looks good since the remodel—an industrial feel with hanging jars and plants. Smooth gray floor and black steel tables and chairs. A few people are with laptops lounging at various spots with coffee, and a tourist taking a photo of her cake on a plate with a travel book in Japanese next to it. Seems like the place to be, I just missed that memo.

Avery made her message clear; she was not going to jump into drinks alone with me. But I'm going to pull an objection to that. She does not get to decide any more of our terms of departure we had in Chicago, because I had let her dictate the terms then for understandable reasons. Enough time has passed that the tables have turned, and my assertive nature has gotten stronger.

Now that I have seen her and know she is within reach, I am not going anywhere. Judging by the bolt of electricity between us when I touched her, I think it's safe to say that there is still something there. How could there not be with our history?

It only took a few sentences with her and I already know. I know she is still a sweet and warm person, and something in me is itching to know if she is still unbelievably fun and wild when she's with me.

There is no way in hell I am letting her slip away again. Five years can be a long time, but it also feels like I saw her just yesterday. The moment her eyes fluttered up to my gaze at Matchbox, it came back.

Everything.

The whole weekend I was going out of my damn mind, and now it's Monday and I'm not going to wait anymore. I walk to the counter next to a glass case full of various baked goods. Cakes, cookies, brownies, everything I remember she used to bake.

"Can I help you?" the young lady with a streak of blue hair behind the counter asks.

"Yeah, uhm, a cappuccino, and maybe you can tell me if Avery is here?" It comes off casually, I hope.

"Yeah, let me check for you." She puts my cup under the coffee machine. I give her my cash and put a tip in the tip jar as she heads off. I look around the place, studying for clues of Avery.

Vaguely, I hear the blue-haired girl say something to Avery in the back. Something along the lines of... *Are you okay? That is the second batch of brownies you destroyed this morning... your mind seems a little lost today... by the way, there is an insanely hot guy here, you know, a Henry Cavill in a button-down shirt type, and he wants to see you.*

Oh, so Avery's mind is also a mess, because that woman never fails when she has a spoon in hand. Or other things in her hand...

A few seconds later, the teenage girl returns.

The kid gives me a fake smile, "Right, so Avery had to go somewhere. Something about a market, bank, or some other adulting thing to do." The girl is mundane with her tone and seems slightly cynical towards me.

"Really?" The skepticism runs strong in my voice, and I know I have a steely look thrown on my face that has won me many cases.

"Uhh," the girl draws out her noise.

I shake my head, and without any further thought, I walk around the display case and head to the kitchen in a strong stride.

The moment I'm in the kitchen, those beautiful blue eyes meet mine as she looks up from a bowl on the table. She drops the wooden spoon, which is the only noise we hear, and her chest is heaving. Her look tells me she was waiting for me even though she seems to be avoiding me. Her eyes blink and I can see she is collecting herself. But I will wait all day, if that's what it takes.

Slowing my pace, I walk to her, already painfully aware that I have an instinct that sparked again the moment I saw her in Matchbox. Slightly possessive, a strong need to protect her, demand her, and care for her, all rolled into one.

She is wearing a long green dress that clings to her body, paired with white converse sneakers that make her dress seem casual. My mind is venturing to what she possibly has on underneath as I catch a glance of a matching green bra, and how good it would be to take her deep while she leaves that bra on.

Shaking my head faintly, I remember I need to keep my head in the game.

"Hi again," her eyes almost twinkle at me as she swallows.

"Avery," I can't figure out if my tone is a warning or if it is still stuck in disbelief that that we share the same air again.

Slowly, I take a few more steps in her direction as she leans against the island table. The suspense of it all is keeping us on edge, because in two seconds, she has no choice. I need to touch her.

After a moment, her eyes soften and her mouth curves slightly up. "I was waiting for this. You to stop by, I mean," she admits as she looks down at the floor.

I'm in her bubble, and my hand gently grabs her arm. "And I will keep coming back until we talk," I confirm what Avery already knows, because this woman knows me. My eyes cannot leave her. Her hair is slightly different than five years ago. I guess I didn't notice the other night since it was up; slightly shorter, still below her shoulders, and beautiful. Still long enough to pull her down to my cock and...

I'm snapped back when she manages to say something.

"I *know* you will keep coming back," she admits as she looks up at me.

"Yet still you avoid me." I lay out the obvious.

"I'm not... I don't know," she admits in defeat.

We are being so ridiculous. My arms wrap around her and pull her flush to me in a hug. Instantly she sinks into my body. Her hair smelling of vanilla, the feeling of her in my arms making me tighten my hold. The sound of her inhaling my scent making me want to hold her face and remind her that it's me.

For a few seconds, we stand there in an embrace. Lost in the moment, feeling one another again. I swear our pulses are syncing.

Slowly she retreats back and looks up at me with a gentle tug on the corners of her mouth.

"You want a coffee? You shouldn't really be back here."

I have to gently smile. "Why, because you don't trust me when you have a spoon in your hand?"

It makes her grin softly. "No. Because health and safety rules."

She scoots me out of the kitchen and indicates her head in the direction of a free table. I head to the table and sit down as she goes to grab my coffee, and one for herself.

As I briefly wait, I notice there is a box of games on the shelf. My guess is that's for people to sit and play with when drinking their coffee. She has checkers. I take a deep breath as that fact makes something in me dance a little in enjoyment, and I normally hate dancing.

Avery returns with two big mugs and a blueberry muffin.

"Am I taste testing again?" I enquire, as it's something I've done many times for her in the past. I give her my charming grin.

"Yes," she says bluntly as she sits down and hands me a fork.

"That isn't fair. Last time we were on a strict calorie-burning and taste-testing regime," I tease, because in Chicago we would counter every piece of cake with a session of intense sex that would leave us sweating.

Avery rolls her lips in and her face turns pink as she grabs her coffee mug.

"Saw the checkers," I indicate by tilting my head to the shelf with games.

She gives me a warm smile. "I like having board games. People can have a coffee of leisure and a game to play. And someone pretty special taught me how to play checkers."

I'm going to take a wild guess that I am that guy. It does something to my restraint.

The conversation feels familiar. *Too familiar.* If it weren't for the fact that there's a different year on the calendar, I would say that no time has passed.

But it has.

"Look," I begin, "suddenly we are thrown back into each other's lives and we won't be able to escape each other. You at least owe me a conversation." I'm firm with her and it throws her off as she knows what I mean. But I'm confident with my words and I take a sip of my coffee... *wow*, that is good coffee.

"I didn't say I wanted to escape you." Her tone is strong as she corrects me and gives me a piercing stare.

Setting the mug down, I add, "I just think we owe it to ourselves to talk." I touch her hand on the table gently. My eyes hold her gaze and my touch makes her draw in a breath.

"I know. But not today. Give me some time," she softly requests.

"You've had five years, Avery," I remind her almost in a hiss.

She loosens from my hands, but still stays facing me. "That's fair, but I don't understand why you would want to speak to me. Shouldn't I be the last person you would want to see?"

A scoff escapes my mouth, and my fingers pinch the bridge of my nose. Quickly I look around and see nobody is taking notice of us. "You really think that? You have no idea how wrong you are." I'm frank with her because she is off-base by a thousand miles.

Her eyes study me, and I can tell she is thinking something, but instead, she bites her lip and lets her head roll to the side slightly. She's about to change the subject, I know her.

"Since this is your first time here, I take it coffee breaks and you don't mix. One of *those* attorneys still?" she pesters with a raised eyebrow and her fingers tap the tabletop.

She always mocked me for working too much. But as that summer progressed, I was spending every spare moment with her and relishing our time together. She lets her hand weave through her hair and it falls in layers.

"True. I work a lot, but not as much. And here we are. You, the new bakery owner in town that everyone mentioned, but oddly enough, never by name."

"And you are the Jake that everyone kept talking about. I just didn't realize you were my Jake."

I am her Jake. My heart aches. It sinks. My heart does everything again that it did when that summer ended.

"I am yours." It comes out subtly and delicately as my eyes stay glued on the view in front of me.

I don't know if she picks up that I mean it truthfully, or if she thinks I am just confirming who I am.

"Since you are the Jake that Lucas and Abby go on about, and you were living under a rock in recent months, then I think we established you are still married to your work?" She seems genuinely interested.

I scratch my upper lip. "Yeah, that's true. No wife. No girlfriend. Not even a goldfish swimming in a bowl. You?" My eyes study her intensely to see if she found relief from me confirming that I am single.

I think I see a twinkle in her eye.

Already I know her answer, because I had Lucas fill me in on every fact he knew about Avery. Yet it still sends my body into a spin of satisfaction when she confirms it.

"No husband. No boyfriend. No puppies sleeping on

the sofa," she admits, and we both pick up on the energy between us and it's like a familiar wind caressing against our skin. It is relief. "So, the single ladies in this town must be dropping at your feet, dying to get in your bed?" That witty bite of hers comes out in her tone, along with a confident crack of a smile, but I'm hoping she just really wants reassurance.

Tilting my head slightly in an angle and letting a half grin form, I tell her, "Maybe. But my bed hasn't had anyone in it." Her eyes look at me with surprise and almost contentment. "I just moved to my new house and I got a new bed." I let my lips quirk as I watch to see if it gives her a rise. She gently shakes her head side to side, but her face is neutral.

We look at each other, letting the silence surround us. I check my watch.

"How is your grandfather?" she asks.

"He's okay, I see him when I can. How's Greg?"

"Yeah, he's Greg. Got married in a small ceremony in Key West a year ago and now lives in Salt Lake City of all places, working lots of nightshifts. We text a lot because his schedule at the hospital doesn't make it easy to call." She takes a sip of her coffee. "I guess you guys didn't stay in touch?" She is trying to put the puzzle pieces together of what happened after we ended.

I shake my head, "No, but to be honest, we weren't that close before I saw you that summer. In college, yeah, but once everyone graduated and moved on, we just lost touch."

"Makes sense. I don't really keep in contact with people from college except for the occasional social media like. But you're close with Lucas and you studied together, I hear."

"True. But that was graduate school, and I went to his wedding to his ex-wife." I tip my head to the side. I shift our conversation. "I'm happy you're doing what you love," I tell her with full honesty.

There is a pause, and she lets her eyes scan me. "Thanks." She looks at me as if she's taking in the reality of who is in front of her again. "So crazy. You have been here this whole time. I guess I was also living under a rock," she admits.

"I guess we weren't really looking for each other." It comes out a bit bleak. Realizing she may take it the wrong way, I add, "Doesn't mean we weren't waiting."

She looks at me surprised and does not seem to know what to say. Instead, she swallows.

"Look, Jake, we will talk, and we will—" she starts, but her gentle face forms a frown as her eyes peer behind me and she quickly stands up. "Oh no," her face drops.

My inner voice drops an *oh no* too because she did not get to finish that key sentence of what we will be doing. I turn around as she jumps forward. Watching as she races to the Labrador/German Shephard-mix plunging for her.

"I am going to kill Nate," she huffs with frustration as she kneels to grab the dog by the collar. Tank is Nate's—the owner of Matchbox next door—dog that he just adopted.

"What's he doing here?" I ask as I get up off the chair and come to her and Tank.

"Being the bane of my existence. So incredibly cute yet a very bad dog," she explains as she tries to calm the dog down, but he just wants to play. Avery is struggling to hide her smile. "He keeps escaping from Matchbox and heading to the kitchen to grab a snack which is a health and safety nightmare."

My thumb scratches the corner of my mouth with my other hand on my hip as I smile at this scene, slightly jealous that the canine is getting more action than me right now.

"I've got to take him back, but I will see you around. Soon." She's in a hurry as she comes to standing and drags the energetic dog behind her.

"Yeah, you will." It comes out soft, so she can barely hear.

She stops and quickly looks over her shoulder as she struggles with the dog she holds by the collar. "Jake," she calls out, and I nod. "You should try the carrot cake. I worked on the recipe once in your kitchen," she smiles, and in turn I must be beaming.

I watch her every move as she walks away, and in my mind, I feel relief that she is single, here, willing to talk... at some point.

A glimmer of a chance sways by.

"Hey, Gramps," I say, grabbing a chair across from him at the small bedside table.

"Jacob, my boy." He sets out some checkers on the board. His eyes are still striking and the wrinkles on his face run deep. "Came to see me living my final days with these souls who think dinner at five is living on the edge?" my grandfather sarcastically says.

"Come on, Gramps, not everyone lives as wild as you." I smile and sit on the chair, admiring how Finn Sutton still takes every day as an adventure, even at his age.

"How's the courtroom?"

I lean back in the chair and cross my arms. "Good. Busy. But I'm now normally less in the courtroom and handling more out-of-court deals."

"Is that what you want?"

"Yeah. Does that disappoint you?" I ask, studying him.

"No. Seeing you pass the bar was my proudest day since marrying your grandmother. So how you want to use your title is up to you," he smirks proudly.

I move a checker across the board. "Feeling okay? They said you've been coughing a little more than normal," I ask, knowing he won't tell me the truth.

"So be it. I'm old. Besides, I have my private supply of scotch to ensure I have help to cure it," he says confidently, and I know he means it, which makes me grin.

Remembering I brought him a box of brownies that I got after Avery had to return the mutt, I set the box on the table.

"Now you have made my day, my boy."

He grabs a brownie with a smile. In turn, I lean back in admiration and let my thoughts get a little lost in who made them.

"You seem different, Jacob. Tell me. Does it have to do with someone who made these delicious brownies with her sweet hands?"

This man always had a way with the ladies. I chuckle as he always amazes me how he can read me.

"Maybe so," I confirm sheepishly.

"Finally, someone new in your life?"

I look around as I get lost in thought. "She isn't new, and to be honest, it's a shock to see her again. Not bad, either. In fact, maybe incredible."

My grandfather gives me that sly grin that gets all the nurses' attention. "Then give her your best charm. How long has it been?"

"Five years since I saw her." I stare into the distance.

"Were you waiting for her?"

I take a few beats to think. "I never knew I was, but now that I see her again, I think I always was," I admit, and I feel a pinch in my heart, that organ that has gone on hiatus every time I was with someone who wasn't Avery.

Before my grandfather can continue his line of questioning, a body lands in the chair next to me.

"Hey there, Gramps. Thought I would stop by," my sister Becca chimes.

My sister Becca is a fast talker and has zero filter. She's wearing black like usual to match her dyed-black hair, yet she doesn't cross the line into goth.

Becca looks at me. "You look a little prickly today. You know, you really should consider going out with Tracy who I've been trying to set you up with. She may lighten your mood." My sister tries to set me up with a lot of women.

"Becca, please don't get into this today. I've had a long weekend," I beg.

Long weekend, sure. It was more like Avery is inescapable in my mind. I ran a longer trail run than my usual, hammered out a few contracts, and even cleared out some boxes that have been sitting in one of my spare rooms for three years. That was a bad fucking move because mementos of her fell out of the box.

That photo and that tiny black box she doesn't even know I have.

The reminders of what we could have had. The reminders of our ending.

"You're a sweet guy who takes care of all of us, especially as Mom and Dad are on their year-long retirement trip across Asia. Wouldn't matter, though, as it's always you who watches out for everyone, and I just want to see you happy. Work a little less, find someone, finally fill that expensive car with kids. Just turn that frown upside down, please," Becca insists.

I shake my head at her.

"I am not taking relationship advice from you. How's the divorce coming along? You touched base with the attorney I recommended? Don't sign anything until I read it through," I remind her. My sister is going through a divorce, and I was never a fan of her soon-to-be ex.

She puffs, "Geez, you're a mood killer."

"Children," Gramps gives us a stern warning.

"Listen, I'm going to go. I know your favorite grandchild is leaving, but I will see you next week again, okay?" I say as I stand up from my chair and pinch my sister's arm.

"Okay. But go charm the one you were waiting for." Gramps smiles.

My sister looks between us before a grin forms, similar to a cat catching a mouse.

"There's a woman?" she asks in delight.

Rubbing my forehead in frustration. "No. Yes. No. Not exactly, well, yes."

Yeah, well done, Jake, really constructing sentences these days.

Holding a hand up to Becca, I request, "Can I please use my token free pass to avoid this conversation with you, Becca?"

Becca claps her hands in joy. "This week, sure. But since you just asked that, then it means we may finally have found the one. So, go use your charm," she grins.

A frustrated exhale escapes me as I leave.

When I get to my car and turn it on, I notice the piece of carrot cake in a box sitting on my car floor. I did what Avery said and took a piece of carrot cake to-go so I could try it. Grabbing the box and the plastic fork, I open the box and tuck in.

The moment the moist cake hits my tongue, it all comes back.

CHAPTER SIX

JAKE: 5 YEARS AGO

"But this is how you wanted me, no?" Avery gives me a knowing grin. She walks slowly backwards towards my bedroom as I follow, her hands pulling my tie.

"You listen very well," I remark, admiring her black heels, stockings with suspenders, and matching black bra with elements of gold. The outfit was made for one purpose only, to say *fuck me*, and it was especially requested by me earlier in the week.

"But didn't you want to bake a cake?"

Her looks are pure seduction. "That can wait."

When we reach my bedroom, she goes to the bed and the mattress dips as she kneels. "Tell me what you want. I listen very well." It rolls off her lips, sultry, and if it were possible to get even harder than steel, then it just happened.

"Come to the edge of the bed," I order as I unbuckle my belt. The sound of it coming undone makes her gulp softly in excitement.

She licks her lips and obliges. Her fingers find my maroon-colored tie and untie it, the feeling of her fingers tugging sending more excitement to my groin. When she gets the tie free, I quickly take the fabric from her hand as we will need it. Her fingers go on to unbutton my shirt, and she kisses my skin after every single button, and it sends sparks through my body. She makes a trail that leads her to under my belly button, where anticipation heats in me as her eyes shoot up to meet mine. Quickly, I move my briefs to the floor, along with my pants.

"Take me in your mouth," I instruct her as my hands grab her hair. Without hesitation, she wraps her lips around my tip then moves to take me fully in her mouth, and I let a groan escape. "You feel so good," I grunt.

That seems to make her enjoy it more. My cock feels like it's drowning in a pool as her mouth gets wetter, and moans vibrate around my flesh as her mouth slides up and down. She is excellent at this; I know because this isn't her first time doing this to me. If I'm not careful, this will end sooner than planned.

My hips move to bring me a little deeper in her mouth, and I feel her reflex react. "You're doing so good," I encourage, her eyes looking up occasionally to check I'm watching her, which is so fucking hot; the feeling that she's looking for approval.

Pulling her hair, I bring her away and her mouth looks to be a gorgeous mess. "I have other plans for you."

"What would that be?" she asks with a raspy voice as her eyes roam over me.

Taking my tie, I grab her wrists and secure the fabric around them, binding them together. Right away, that sexy grin of satisfaction flashes across her face as she willingly tests the knot with a tug. She enjoys it. It drives me crazy that our minds are so in tune together. We know what the other wants and likes because it is the same.

"You are going to lie down," I tell her as I guide her

down on the bed, putting her bound wrists above her head. My mouth goes straight to her breast where I move the fabric of her bra to the side so my mouth can cover a nipple. My want for her urges me to suck her taut bud relentlessly. Her moan escapes and her thighs spread open from enjoyment.

"Don't stop," she begs.

My fingers play with her other nipple, and after giving both breasts the attention they deserve, my mouth drags down her flat stomach to her panties. She is soaking, and when my mouth goes over her clit with the thin layer of lace between us, I can taste her subtle sweetness. A magic potion that makes me let go of all my inhibitions.

Her moans escaping and body arching to my mouth tells me she is in her own world of ecstasy, and I love that I am doing that to her.

I lose count of how many times she pants *please, so good,* and *I want you in me.* But I get the message and move the fabric aside so I can let my fingers explore her warm wet flesh, and let my tongue reach her sweet spot. Her legs wrap around my neck and her back arches as her hands stay bound above her. She has become powerless and cannot lie still. I'm driving myself insane with the feeling of power I have over her.

After a few minutes of teasing her, she quickly tremors and shakes under my tongue. My head moves slowly back up her body, and I marvel at the view in the process.

"You taste so fucking good, Ave," I whisper as I look at her red and glowing face. My mouth finds her neck again to kiss her vigorously there, teasing her skin between my teeth, as my fingers continue to pump in and out of her warm center.

"I'm so wet for you," she admits barely through a whisper as she seems to be floating in her desire.

"You are so wet, which is good, because you're going to go to your hands and knees so I can take you from behind."

She gives me a droll smile as she slowly rolls to her side then adjusts her body so she is resting on her knees and bound arms, her gorgeous ass in the air.

Positioning myself behind her, I rub a hand over her ass that is perfectly on display between the straps of her stockings. The tip of my length trails along her skin until it finds her wetness, rubbing along her sex and clit. Slowly I slide into her until I am deep. I want to get lost in her. Her head dances with her bound hands as she moans, and I find a rhythm in her as I grip her hips in place, making her moan and writhe. The music she is making with her sounds encourages me to keep going. Hell, I could do this to her all day, over and over again.

She makes a small yelp every time I hit her deep in that spot that I know can make her scream.

"You feel so, so *good*," she cries.

"I want you to come, babe."

"I only want to come if you come," she declares.

That nearly does it to me. My hands reach under her to massage her clit, cup her breasts and touch her everywhere as I pick up the pace.

When her internal walls tighten around me as she begins to tremble, panting my name in a hoarse voice, it sends me to new heights until I find release.

As I come down from our high, I rub her back gently with my hand. Pulling out, I fall on the bed with her and spoon her from behind, feeling her breathing pace attempt to steady.

"That was *sooo* good," she comments lazily as she lies in her frenzy, and I smile at her admission.

My lips kiss her shoulder. "I love it when you come," I whisper.

Avery hums in response. "I love doing what you tell me," she confesses, and I kiss her shoulder again.

After a pause, I look at her and take in the view of her in my bed. She looks like she belongs here.

"Do I now live in your tie or...?" she asks coyly with an amused look, indicating to her wrists above her head that she shakes slightly.

I let out a chortle as my hands go to untie her wrists. When she's free, she readjusts her position so she can lie on her back and look up at me lying on my side.

I realize in all our fantasy-making tonight that I did not kiss her. Not on the lips anyway. That intimate act. Her soft full lips that meet mine, always with thirst.

It should not matter anymore as we already had our release. But my eyes stare at her mouth and I don't hesitate as I dive onto her mouth with mine. It catches her by surprise, but very quickly she returns the kiss, with her now-free hands coming to my face as we kiss deeper. Time stills when we kiss, I can never kiss her hard enough.

Pulling away, her lip twitches with a not-so-secret smile and her eyes have a flicker.

In that moment, I know I cannot get enough of her.

"ARE YOU SURE I'M NOT INTERRUPTING YOUR DAY? I mean, it seems like you have a lot of work to do... *on a Saturday*." Avery gives me a knowing look as she pours flour

into a bowl. I offered her my kitchen since it's more prac-
tical than where she's staying.

"Nah, it's fine. You can do your thing and I will work at
the table over there. I have my Bluetooth on, anyhow." I
motion to my dining table, where I just want to do a few
things on my laptop as I'm in the middle of discovery for a
case.

I walk to her and let my arms wrap around her from
behind. "Plus, you deserve your baking bliss after what you
did with my tie last night and what just transpired in here."
I kiss her neck.

After last night with the tie, then waking to find her in
my work shirt and nothing else as she cooked me eggs in the
kitchen... It sent us straight to the kitchen floor for a quick
workout.

She softly giggles as she tries to shake me away and
focus on her stirring.

I have seen her a few times this week, normally meeting
at my place when I'm returning from a long day at the office
and heading straight to bed.

Not to sleep.

And to be honest, we normally wouldn't fall asleep until
about one after chatting about travel, music, dream houses,
family, and what work would be like if we each had our
dream career scenario.

It is a natural current between us.

Now that I have her in my kitchen in my shirt and bare
legs, I don't want to work. I want to have her on the counter.

"Okay, well, I will get my cake in the oven then give you
some space. I can work on my laptop in your room."

My arm reaches for her as she finishes putting the cake
in the oven. "Yeah, but you know what? I don't have so
much work to do. Want to watch a movie or something?"

Her eyes widen in surprise "You? Not working on a Saturday morning? Have shapeshifters taken over your body?" she muses.

"I don't know, maybe you need to test my body," I tease as I bring an arm around her waist and press her body to mine.

She considers and then surprises me when she asks, "Maybe you could teach me how to play checkers?"

I did not see that coming. To be honest, a movie was also a cover as I thought maybe we could do something along the lines of my counter, shower, and bed. But her suggestion sounds good right about now.

"Sure."

"Okay, but you have to actually teach me. I forgot how to play."

Fuck, that sentence sends bad thoughts through my brain. Dirty thoughts. And in this moment, I am regretting not having a contact sport like football as the hobby to teach her. But my brain manages to tell my body to calm down, and for the next two hours, we laugh over checkers. I forgot how hanging out with someone over something so simple as checkers can be enjoyable.

When she dashes off to the open kitchen to finish decorating her cake, a thought floats in my head when I realize she is going to make someone an incredibly happy husband one day. That thought came out from the left field in my brain, and I make a mental note to drink an extra beer tonight with the guys as I may need it.

"Ready." She beams, setting a pecan on the white iced two-tier cake, holding up a plate to me.

"Whoa, that looks very good." I slowly walk to her and let my arm wrap around her waist.

She kisses my wrist as she brings the spoon of the icing

to my mouth. I let out a sound when I taste the cream cheese frosting, then groan when I watch her lick the same spoon.

Fuck, she can lick. Other things too.

Her facial expression tells me she knows where my mind is going.

"You have a dirty mind," she confirms, studying me with a sexy look.

I hold up my hands innocently and we both laugh before she cuts a piece of cake and takes a fork, bringing it to my mouth.

"Whoa, that is good. What's in this magic stuff?" I ask.

She smiles with pride. "Crushed pineapple, carrots, the usual, and I am experimenting with spices. Cloves, actually."

"You really should look into opening your own bakery," I encourage her as I take another bite of the cake.

Her shoulders sink. "Maybe. But if I look into opening my own bakery, then you should look into starting your own practice," she orders as she tugs my shirt away from my chest.

"Are you trying to negotiate a deal?" I ask with a humorous grin.

"Perhaps I should. We both work too much." It trails off into the air.

"I get to keep this cake, right?" I gleam, because this is some damn good cake.

"Yeah, but I'm not sure I put enough icing on it," she tilts her head in different angles, studying the cake in front of her.

Letting my finger grab some icing from the bowl, I wipe it on her neck.

"I could think of somewhere else where we can put

some icing." I go in and lick the icing off her neck and she lets out a whimper, all the while she is grabbing at my t-shirt.

"Jake. NO. That will be a sticky mess," she laughs. Her laugh is adorable. Infectious. It makes me want to smile, even if it's a bad day.

"So, we can take a shower—together," I continue to tease her neck. But she manages to escape my hold.

"You are *very good* in the shower. But maybe another time. I need to go, actually." This disappoints me and she picks up on it and slaps my shoulder gently. "I really want to check out Navy Pier and maybe walk endlessly around a museum. My colleague said we could meet up since she also wants to check out some sights. I've been in the city a few weeks, and so far, I have seen my office and every angle of your place. That's it."

Every angle of my place is the only place in town she needs to know. But even I know the girl deserves the whole Chi-town experience.

"I get it." I keep her hand in mine as she stretches her arms to reach for her phone to text her colleague. I reel her in back towards me. "You should go meet up with your colleague. But maybe I can take you for deep-dish pizza tonight after I meet the guys for a drink?" I realize I am entering dangerous territory, and to be honest, I normally don't do this. But Avery is different, I enjoy our conversations.

She looks at me and tries not to let a smile show. "That sounds tempting, but I don't want to let Sarah down."

Because under this vixen is a person with a warm heart. Doesn't take a genius to see that.

There's an awkward silence between us as she bites her

lip. I let her hand go so she can go change. But as she walks away, she stops and turns to me.

"I actually have these Cubs tickets from work, if you want to come. I know you hate to part from your work before 9pm, but it's a night game later in the week." I can see she's not sure if it's okay to ask, considering the rules of our arrangement. And sometimes I feel like she looks to me for the answers as I maybe have more experience when it comes to sex. But this is not sex. This is two people wanting to spend time together. And I do not even second-guess it when I say yes.

By end of the week, we are sitting in jeans and Cubs shirts in excellent seats at Wrigley Field, compliments of her office, watching the Cubs lead the Brewers, enjoying a beer and hotdog, talking about baseball because she has no clue.

Every time she has a question, she squeezes my arm and keeps our arms interlaced.

Every time the Cubs hit the ball, she nuzzles her head into my shoulder because she can't look.

Every time she lets out a sarcastic remark, I give her a knowing look.

Because I know her now. More than just intimately.

I know how she hates unmade beds, pretentious bakeries, and some of my musical tastes. How she teases me about the fact I work a lot and how she likes to watch me work at my table. How rainy nights are her favorite. And when she asks for the time, she looks at my watch with a warm smile because she likes the fact it has a story. And how when she bakes, she's in her own world. I know all of these things, because I know her.

And I do not want it to stop.

Her colleague comes to sit next to us as she arrives late to the game.

"Hey, Sarah. This is Jake. Jake, Sarah." Avery motions between us. We both say hi to each other. She seems like a decent gal, my age and lives locally.

"A good game," Sarah comments. "Normally baseball bores me to death. Hope you're enjoying the game, Avery. Cubs fans can get a little crazy."

"Yeah? I think Chicago people get a little crazy with any Chicago team." Avery cracks out a laugh.

"Ah well, at least you have a boyfriend to show you around. Bars around here celebrate like crazy if the Cubs win."

"Oh, well, Jake isn't—" Avery looks lost for what to say and how to correct Sarah on the boyfriend comment. I wrap an arm around Avery's shoulder.

"Yeah, Jake will show her around," I reiterate. Avery just looks at me with a death stare and a smile she is trying to hide.

"Hope the rain will hold off. Rain delays are no fun," Sarah says.

"It's supposed to rain? How did I miss that?" Avery asks, and there's a hint of excitement in her voice, which makes me smile and tighten my arm around her.

The Cubs do win, and when we leave, the skies open with rain. Someone above is being good to me tonight. Especially as it's not sprinkling, it's full-on need-to-run-for-safety open skies. This only makes Avery laugh more. A contagious laugh.

"Come on," I yank her with a smile as we head away

from the crowds exiting the stadium. No way we will grab a cab in this. I know a place we can have a quiet drink, hidden away. The rain picks up as we walk, and I see a covered detour. Motioning to her, I pull us into the alley with a green awning. My pull was strong enough that she lands against my chest. We're soaked from the rain and it just makes her laugh more.

My long finger and thumb reach under her chin and tilt her head up so she's looking at me, my mouth in particular. My hands move to clasp her cheeks and she brings her lips to my inner wrist for a gentle kiss before turning her mouth back in my direction, her eyes looking up to me with a sparkle.

"You always kiss my wrist," I mention softly.

"I don't know why. Maybe for the memory of mezcal in your kitchen. Maybe for the fact that it's where you keep your watch that is so important to you. Your wrist is a special spot. I like it," she explains easily and innocently.

Looking into each other's eyes, we both revel in this moment. There is only one thing we want. Our mouths come crashing together for a kiss. Not just any kiss, but a long lingering and deep kiss. When we pull gently apart for air, our eyes meet.

The plan needs to change. She is too enjoyable to be just a fling.

CHAPTER SEVEN

AVERY

"A LITTLE MORE TO THE RIGHT AND MOVE IT CLOSER TO the middle," I indicate to Nate with my camera in hand. He listens and moves the cocktail to the position. It's late afternoon on a weekday and there are only a few people in Matchbox as they get ready for the evening crowd. A mix of indie folk music is playing on the speakers.

"Thanks so much for helping me with my Instagram photos, especially after Tank destroyed your cookie batch. I never knew there's a whole world of Instagram and cocktails. I guess it's good marketing. And when I saw your cake photos and heard you used to work at a marketing firm, then I figured you could help," he explains.

In truth, I could use every distraction I can get. Memories of Jake have been playing on a loop in my head. My body wants one thing, my mind is going in all directions, and my poor little heart is making me feel things I thought I'd recovered from. I am not avoiding Jake. I'm just scared of what will happen when we talk or we fu—

Okay, Avery, own it. Ugh, I *am* avoiding Jake.

I just do not know how to be around him.

How do I do this? That man changed my life. Now I carry around a souvenir of guilt and I don't know how to make it right. And I want to make it right. I wonder if this is going to be a long process of fixing and repairing? And what do I do if he wants neither? We have so much to catch up on, so much to discuss. We could be two different people. Time does things.

My. Head. Is. A. Mess.

The last few days, I have been running an extra mile to clear my head in the mornings, baked extra cookies to relieve stress, and admittedly looked at some old photos on my phone that were buried in the cloud. Shock wore off and turned to a mix of excitement and desire.

Hope. It turned to hope.

Focusing on the task at hand, I look at Nate with a smile. "No problem. And since you are repaying me by telling me the secret for getting the lemon supplier at a discounted rate, then consider us even." I grab the next cocktail and position it.

"Again, I am so sorry about Tank. I know it has happened a few times now, but he's going to a dog trainer every week," Nate apologizes as he lets his thumb scratch his cheek.

Nate is a great guy, just not my kind of guy. But as a friend and fellow local business owner, then he is at the top of the list. And with his looks, I am certain there's a list of women waiting for him to rock their world.

Taking my ankle boots off, I'm left with my skinny jeans and black V-neck shirt with lace edging. My hair is down, and I have a few bracelets on my left wrist. I hop on the bar. "That sounds promising, I guess."

"What are you doing?" he asks, amused.

Standing on the bar, I lean over the lemon-colored cocktail in a tall glass with a lime on the edge. "I need a better angle and it's good to have a few photos from an above angle. How many more cocktails do we have?" I ask, busy with the camera. Just like I do at the bakery, I take one day and do all the photos for the coming weeks.

"Two more. Maybe these two should go together?" He brings another similar-looking cocktail with a different glass next to it.

Immediately, I get on all fours to get a better viewpoint.

"You really are amazing at this," Nate adds.

"Amazing on a table, she is," that recognizable voice announces from behind me. "Is she a new feature of the place? Because it is quite a view."

I can guess what look is probably thrown on his face. I have a library of options.

My stomach jumps from this unexpected visitor, and my heart rate surging makes me think I need to upgrade my insurance plan to include spontaneous heart failure. I freeze a little before turning my head slightly to look behind me and find Jake standing there. His eyes hazed and face firm, yet his slight glare tells me he is enjoying the view. *Really* enjoying the view.

Brushing off his comment, I focus again on the task at hand and stand up on the bar again. "Last one, right, Nate?"

Nate changes the drinks and doesn't seem to pick up on the fact that Jake is watching us with a hardened look. I'm not even wondering why he is here in the middle of the business day. That's not the guy I remember.

"Hey, man, thanks for coming. Just give me five minutes to finish with Avery and then we can look at the contracts," Nate informs Jake, and I have my answer about why Jake is here. Something business related.

My eyes cannot help but look at Jake who is loosening

his tie. *Damn*, that move can make me feel like liquid in one second flat. He doesn't seem too thrilled that Nate and I are interacting, and it gives me butterflies as I always liked his protective nature.

"Sure," he responds, short. Our eyes meet and there is some tension, if I have to be honest. Just can't figure out if it is anger or sexual.

"You know what, guys? I think I'm done," I inform them.

"Are you sure?" Jake says. "You should stay and have a drink. I'm sure we can get you a glass of mezcal or *a bottle*." Jake's lips twist in at the corners.

Ah, so it is sexual tension.

My eyes lock with his as I briefly let my mind remember our first weekend together. My head giving him the gentlest of shakes as my jaw moves to the side in slight delight.

Realizing that I am standing on a bar and one of the men in front of me may just be undressing me with his eyes, I snap into action mode.

"Right. So, I'm just going to get down if someone can help?" I ask with uncertainty in my voice, as to who will be my hero of the hour.

Nate is about to open his mouth and offer a hand, but he does not have a chance.

"I've got this, Nate," Jake insists as he motions his hand for Nate not to move. Nate doesn't question it and quickly heads off to somewhere.

Stepping to the ledge of the bar, Jake's hands are waiting for me. As soon as our hands touch and I bend down, he steps closer. Letting his strong arms wrap around my waist as he pulls me close and off the bar. We press together as my body slowly grinds down his. By the laws of science—of course—my arms wrap around his neck. Our eyes meet.

It's warm, it's comfortable, and rushes of memories of how he touches me returns. Most of all, this encounter sends a confirmation to me that he still makes my blood boil with anticipation and desire. Briefly, I get to drown in the intensity that I share with this man when we are sharing the same air.

And he knows this. He knows this because I don't let go when I could have ten seconds ago.

Whispering into my ear, he asks, "This is familiar, no?"

Gulping his smell of fresh spring and feeling his breath, I hide my tremble within me. My eyes look up to him.

"Jake," I give him a playful warning.

He interrupts me before I can continue. "Cloves?"

A smile forms on my mouth because I know he tried my cake. "Yeah. For that extra kick," I admit with my fist making a little gesture. It is only then that I notice I am still in his embrace and my hands have found their way to his hard chest, as I gently claw his crisp white shirt.

He remembers that day in his kitchen where I made a carrot cake while we talked and played checkers, after doing so many other things.

My fingers walk up his tie, and I know I am giving him a smoldering look as I peer up to his eyes.

"Like the tie today. I'm sure it is good for many things." Okay, that line just flew past my filter and it was a *little* sultrier than I intended.

His tongue circles inside his mouth in delight and his grin tells me he feels a slight victory.

Just like that, I remember that if we eventually talk, then a little flirtation is maybe okay. Because that is how we have always been together, and it seems that hasn't changed. That gives me comfort.

Before Jake has the chance to return a counter remark, Nate returns.

Jake and I instantly pull away after our moment, giving each other a knowing look of our eyes clouding with want. I can't be imagining it.

Nate hands me a paper. "Here is the supplier number and all the information. Thanks again for your help, and I promise you Tank is in the doghouse for the rest of the week. You know, if you want someone to look over your supplier contracts, Jake here sometimes helps me out with that stuff." Nate explains this with only good intentions as he has no clue the full history that I have with the man in a suit next to him.

Taking the piece of paper from him, I bite my lip. "I know, Nate. Jake and I know each other, remember?"

Jake has a wry smile. "Probably too much conflict of interest there."

"Oh right, sorry. I forgot my bar is the magical place for reunions." Nate grins.

"My guess is Jake's hourly rate is too expensive for me anyhow," I say, not letting my eyes leave Jake.

A sly smirk forms on Jake's face as he holds our gaze. "I am sure we can work out a mutually beneficial arrangement for that." That was sizzling with sexual innuendo, that I am sure of.

Nate clears his throat, clearly catching on.

Bringing the paper up to the air, I speak. "Thanks, Nate. Anyhow, I will leave you two to your meeting."

As I turn around to leave, I don't get far. Jake calls out my name and I turn to look at him.

"Drinks tonight?" he asks, calm and patient. As if he doesn't want to push me, yet he is hopeful.

"Yeah, sounds good. I'm meeting Jess anyways at the bar on Fifth, so maybe 8?" I give him a warm smile.

His hand reaches for my face and he lets his knuckles graze along my cheek. "It will be good to really catch up with you." It comes out so honest that it makes me want to count the seconds until I see him again, and that is only to talk.

***

After heading home to my apartment to quickly change, I put on a long, casual, blue cotton dress with buttons, tights, ankle boots, and I leave my hair down. I carefully chose my outfit. *Just in case.*

The thought of our good times overwhelms me. The thought of his hands owning me, lips devouring me, and our long talks crosses my mind, always has.

When I looked in the mirror earlier before I arrived at the bar, I could not help remembering the overbearing fact that time has passed. And that is okay, I like who I am now. But I do not know what time has done to him, or us. People change, and it's been five years.

Sitting across the low table from Jess, I am enjoying drinks at the hotel on Fifth. Not only a hotel, but a great restaurant and lounge. Oversized sofas and a crackling fire in the fireplace make the atmosphere warm. The type of place you would want to have a cozy break during a day of skiing, or a weeknight glass of wine with a past lover.

I'm not a fan of clichés, but this place nails it for tonight.

After talking about how fast Sam, Jess's toddler, is growing and debating what is wrong with the new design of our local organic food market, Jess changes the topic to my business.

"By the way, I heard you are up for a Sagey—the award for best local business."

"Oh yeah, I heard something about that. What a ridiculous name for an award, yet slightly catchy," I admit, taking a sip of wine.

Jess holds her hand up. "That's a big thing, you should be excited."

And I should be. I have worked hard re-designing the place yet ensuring the old customers stay happy. I've added healthy and vegan options to the menu, experimented with different baked goods, created a following on social media to build hype around the menu. And even I cannot be modest at how popular weekend breakfast is at the place.

But my mind is somewhere else this week. Preoccupied with someone else. My face must show it as Jess looks to me with understanding.

"Jake?" she asks with her forehead furrowing.

As I nod a slow yes, and Jess gives me a knowing smile.

"What's the deal? The way you two looked at one another the other night at Matchbox, I thought for sure you would have left together to, well..." Jess grins as she tips the wine bottle upside down above her glass to get the last drop.

I'm amused. "You mean have amazing sex that leaves me ruined for all other men?" I offer as I lean against my arm that is propped against the back of the sofa.

"Something tells me you have some good memories tucked in your head."

Licking my lips, I admit, "I do. Really, I do. I mean, sex with Jake was *wow*. We had incredible sexual chemistry." I get a little lost in my mini confession.

"Okay. You're single and he's single, so why not, you

know? It's what I did, and I ended up with a husband," Jess grins.

The idea of Jake as my husband sends an aching feeling between my legs that first stops at my heart.

"We have a lot to talk about. At first, I was in so much shock to see him again that my brain couldn't process. But I don't need more time, and that is why I am here waiting to have drinks with Jake. And I hope I can find restraint; I mean, it has been a while for me. That attraction is still there, for sure—or least I think it is—and he has this way of just taking the lead, so yeah, I don't trust myself around him in that way. But I don't know how to be around him, because we did end, and maybe that's the way it was supposed to be." I take a sip of my wine.

"Sex then talking after is not an option?" Jess grins.

I shrug, "I am trying to use my brain."

"Can I ask why you two didn't work out?" Jess innocently asks as she turns her wine glass by the stem.

Pausing, I tap the bottom of my glass. "You know, that topic is for another day. Just, we started out as sex only, *really* good sex, and it turned into more. We were together only a summer, but even so, I had a glimpse of a future with him. The timing wasn't right, and plans changed. Can I ask what it was like for you to reconnect with someone after time apart?" Because if memory serves me right, she did not see Leo for quite some time.

Jess smiles to herself and leans her head to the side. "Well, it's complicated. We have a child together, so we were always bound to reconnect. If I could hit replay, I would have been open about my feelings from the moment we laid eyes on each other again. In case you didn't notice, I am definitely team reconnect-and-see-what-happens."

"I think I am too, but that's not my decision to make,

and I'm not sure he would want to, or if I can be what he needs," I confess.

I wonder what reconnecting with Jake will be like. Will it feel like we haven't had a five-year pause? Because I still dream about those nights with him, lying in his arms. I'm not sure we can be only friends. It's too complicated.

No matter the scenario that is destined for us, I still struggle with the fact that I walked away.

"Come on, Ave. Join team reconnect and have amazing make up sex." Jess smiles as she nudges my arm.

"Okay, you are convincing," I deadpan with a soft smile.

"That may be good because I think they have arrived." Jess gives me a funny look as her head indicates to the door.

Turning my head to follow her line of sight, I see that Jake has arrived with Leo. He didn't notice me as they quickly go to the bar. Jake is still as striking as I remember, even out of a suit, in dark blue jeans and a forest-green button-down shirt. His watch on show from his partially rolled sleeves.

"Ready for this?" Jess asks sincerely and places a reassuring hand on my shoulder.

Taking a breath, I look up, knowing very well his eyes will be waiting for mine.

CHAPTER EIGHT

AVERY: 5 YEARS AGO

"THAT WAS A GOOD SET, BUT THE VIC ALWAYS HAS GOOD shows," Jake explains as we get off the elevator to his place after arriving back from a concert.

"Definitely a good night, and I think I know how to make it better," I tell him as he unlocks his door.

"Oh yeah?" His interest is piqued. I nod with a grin.

As soon as we get into his place, I yank his arm and drag him with me to the kitchen. I throw some music on the Bluetooth and grab a plate of brownies from the fridge— because I've taken over his fridge. I'm spending a lot of time with him lately. Yet still, every time we see each other, it is exhilarating.

"Your night just got better," I say slowly and give him a peck on the lips with my hands cradling his face before quickly pulling away to grab two glasses for the chilled mezcal with lemonade in the fridge. My body moves to the music on the speakers, hips swaying side to side as I twirl on the balls of my feet. I bring the bottle to the plate of brownies on the counter.

Jake is standing there, leaning against the counter watching me, taking in the view.

"My night did just get better it seems. You're in a good mood. Kind of playful."

"I am happy... and playful," I confess, handing him a glass of mezcal and a brownie.

When he lets out a satisfying moan from the decadent chocolate brownie he bites into, it makes me laugh. "I'm getting deeply concerned that my baking makes you moan more than me."

He places the brownie and drink on the counter, then his arms quickly circle around my waist and he pulls me close and tight to his body. "Can't lie, it's a competition. But you do something on a whole different level," he growls into my neck.

I pinch his stomach, so he steps away and lets out a curse.

Taking a sip from my drink and going back to dancing, I begin to dance bigger movements around the kitchen and into the living room. He is following me, and I know he isn't a dancer, but I admire that he keeps smiling and stays near.

In my zone, I continue to dance and sway to the music with drink in hand.

"I'm crazy about you."

I stop in my tracks to look at him, and his face is dead serious. My face goes back to neutral as I set my drink down.

Quickly, I glide a step forward trying to close our distance. I stop my huge grin from spreading across my face that would make me struggle to speak. "I'm absolutely crazy about you too."

His face turns to a look that would make the sun feel

inadequate. "Come here," he demands, and I take the step closer.

As soon as we touch, his mouth engulfs mine in a firm, passionate, and claiming kiss. When we pull back to breathe, he turns me around to face away from him, and an inferno spreads between us quickly. He pushes me against the floor-to-ceiling window overlooking the city. Taking my hands, he places them above my head against the glass, and then his hands grip my hips. In one jerk, he pulls my hips close to him. Every movement has a purpose. My back arches down and I'm in a 90-degree angle when his mouth comes to my ear.

"So incredibly crazy about you," he hisses through his teeth as one hand goes up my dress, and the other cups my covered breast.

"Show me," I beg, breathless.

And he does.

ALL I HAD TO DO WAS KNOCK ON HIS DOOR AFTER WORK, say it was the weekend, and he had me wrapped around him in record time, with my summer dress hiked up on my waist as he set me on the kitchen counter.

"I've been thinking about this all day." My voice is ragged as we both move vigorously.

"I know. You told me, because you have a dirty mouth," he breathes into my ear. Because I may have sent him a dirty text during the day... or three.

"Really? My not-so-innocent texts are the problem? You're the one who filmed what we did last night," I tease him as we both pick up our pace. I have no limits with Jake, and that's a first.

"You loved every second of it," he groans into my ear as we both begin to fall down the rollercoaster together.

Soon we are both seeing stars and support each other as we come down from our elevated bliss.

As he is still inside me and we are both still recovering, it slips off his lips so easily and casually. "I'm taking you to dinner," he states, and it comes out sweet. Jake does not mean a casual dinner between friends who are sleeping together. His eyes tell me it's the kind of dinner that women dream of with someone they enjoy.

At first, I'm taken aback, but when the guy who makes your head spin is inside you, having just made you come, you are defenseless. And I break a rule.

"Okay." It comes out floaty as there is an internal smile happening in my body.

Then we kiss a simple confirmation kiss that makes us both grin like two giddy teenagers.

Half an hour later, we are walking to dinner hand in hand because our electricity just draws us to do it. But I can't help letting my mind go to where it has been a lot recently. What is happening with us? Why do stars feel like they're shooting, and no one exists in this city of 2.5 million people except me and him? How is it that I feel like I know every little thing about him? The way he takes his watch off, the way he chews a pen when he's working... How he has a protective streak that makes him drape an arm around me anytime someone passes near me. The way he holds me tenderly until I fall asleep. I cannot get enough of him. All my boundaries have been crossed... and I'm enjoying the other side.

"Still no openings at your company's branch in Chicago for after your project?" he asks, as I mentioned it before.

"No. A shame, really." I don't like what I'm saying and the look on his face tells me he doesn't either.

"Right," he responds distantly.

There is an awkward silence, but then abruptly his hand cups the back of my neck and he pulls me to his mouth. A needy and possessive kiss, which I gladly give back. Almost as if we are trying to forget the fact that our agreement has an expiration date.

Pulling away, we both have a weakened smile, knowing this will all come to an end at some point.

"We are breaking a few rules, aren't we?" I continue to walk but let my eyes sideline to Jake, my face full of anticipation.

"You mean Cubs games, dinners, and romantic walks?" he shoots out knowingly as if he predicted my words.

"Yeah, something like that."

"We ventured beyond sex only, but is it breaking a rule if the clients are both in agreement?" he asks, looking at me as we stop walking. My face turns away as I want to hide my delight.

"I'm leaving by the end of the summer," I remind him.

"I'm still a workaholic," he tries to assure me.

"So what do we do?" I drag out.

"We have a good summer enjoying each other, being together?" he offers with a slightly hitched voice and a shrug, his hand in one pocket, suit jacket hanging over a shoulder by a finger on the other hand. It's as if he's afraid of my answer, which crosses the line to swoon-worthy, as this man does not do anything but confident.

"Sounds fun, but complicated," I admit.

These are dangerous waters, and I'm not sure I have a life vest for this. But I can't turn away, I don't want to. I will learn to swim better.

"Could be. You can also walk away now, ending our original idea of fun," he prompts me, and I can see on his face that he's hoping that I say no way.

We begin to walk again.

He holds my arm tighter and I lean my head against his shoulder when I say, "I should walk away, but I don't want to. Let's have a good summer."

His body relaxes, as does mine. He kisses my hair as he pulls me. "Maybe we'll get a sign that it can be more, maybe not," he mentions softly. I kiss his inner wrist that hangs around my shoulder as I break away from his hold and entwine our hands.

That line is full of hope that maybe we both see this as more than a fling. Because I feel something for him, and by the way his body responds to my touch, it tells me he feels something too. I cannot get enough of him. He makes me go senseless, makes me smile, holds me, warms me, cares for me, makes me laugh—and not just that, but I want to do all of that to him. Maybe it's love, maybe it's lust. It has me thinking crazy ideas as in 'you want to try long-distance until I have a new job in Chicago' kind of crazy.

But I say nothing, and we continue to walk as I take in his philosophy.

Because the problem with signs is they push you in directions you least expect.

CHAPTER NINE

AVERY

MY MIND BREAKS AWAY FROM THE MEMORY WHEN JESS nudges my arm as Leo and Jake approach us.

"Hope you don't mind if I steal my wife away, seems we need to go home to the sitter... who is sick." Leo has a wry smile on his face.

I know they're ditching us so Jake and I can be alone. "No problem at all," I reply.

"Why don't you two finish the bottle of wine?" Jess offers a bit shakily as she slides up and off the sofa to join her husband. Indicating her head towards Jake and giving me bulging eyes.

Leo slaps a hand on Jake's shoulder as he walks away. "We'll finish going over the contract another time," he says faintly with a knowing grin.

Jake's gaze does not leave me, but he nods slightly to Leo in amusement of their play.

"They were subtle," he notes with one hand in his pocket, and I have to smile. Jake scratches his upper lip with his thumb. "Still okay for drinks alone with—"

Quickly and without hesitation, I interrupt and reach

up to grab his arm. "The wine bottle is actually finished. Jess's doing, not mine, I swear. But do you want another drink?"

He instantly nods yes, sliding next to me on the sofa, checking me out in the process, and it is not just my imagination. He leans in and kisses my cheek innocently. Offering me the chance to inhale his scent, which may just be some magic potion he brewed up.

"Hi." He has a sexy smile as he pulls away.

I look at him, and I am sure my eyes are twinkling. "Hi."

This is *not* going to be easy.

"Tonight, I just want to hear how you've been the last few years." I am honest and make it clear that talking about our ending does not seem right in this moment.

"And I want to hear the same from you." He gives me that charming smile where I can see his dimples. He indicates for the waiter to come take our order and we order a whiskey neat for him and a gin and tonic for me.

"Did Nate's supplier help you out?"

I appreciate his effort to break the ice. "I haven't called yet. I'll do it tomorrow. What brought you to Matchbox on a weekday? Shouldn't you be slaying someone in a courtroom or something? Oh wait, sorry, I shouldn't ask. Client confidentiality and all."

He laughs, "Slaying in courtrooms? Is that the image you still have of me? And true, I can't talk about my clients. But I can tell you what I'm up to. I decided to invest into the Matchbox brand." He is studying me for my response.

A sound of surprise escapes me. "Investing in an alcohol brand? You?" There is disbelief in my voice, because this guy works too much to have time for anything but work and sex.

Slanting a shoulder, the corner of his mouth lifts. "Yeah,

why not? It's fun and I like the idea behind it. In ten years, I will be the cool uncle to my niece; the uncle that partially owns a brand of alcohol."

A laugh escapes me, and I nod my approval. "Well, this *is* a surprise, and it sounds kind of awesome. Seems you are broadening your horizons outside of legal documents."

"My life is a little different since I moved from Chicago, true. Having my own law practice also means I have more flexibility for this kind of stuff."

After getting our drinks, he tells me how he decided he wanted a slower pace of life. Working in a big firm had cost a lot of hours of personal time and he wanted to be closer to his family. How passing the state bar in Colorado went faster than he expected. How he goes for trail runs nearby and always tries carrot cake if it's on the menu somewhere, because I got him hooked.

Nudging him slightly in the thigh with mine, I enlighten him. "I'm surprised you're not married yet. I mean, mid-thirties is hitting your peak," I tease and let my eyes widen in amusement as my finger circles the rim of my glass.

"I mean, I dated, maybe a lot. Nothing serious and nothing lately, but I didn't find anyone with the same spark."

Does he mean the same spark as me? My heart jumps.

"I get it. I tried to date in the last few years, but there was always something missing. Couldn't be open with them. Not like with you. You know all my secrets," I remark before taking a sip of my drink then suddenly stop mid-sip as I realize what I just said. Slowly, I let my glass return to the table and my eyes look up at him. He nods with his eyes piercing me with understanding.

The moment between us is heavy and this could go

many ways. But he smiles and brings us back to neutral territory, the way he could always so easily do.

"And how did you end up with Smokey Java's?"

"I was really done with my job in marketing. I had buried myself in work after, well—"

"You were done with it when you were in Chicago already," he interrupts as he pushes up his sleeves. I appreciate that we moved past my little blip.

"Yeah, true, and then Abby mentioned this bakery near her was going on the market. I had a peek at it when I was visiting family. After living in San Francisco where everything is extortionate in price, the costs saved by moving here was ideal, and it got me far enough so that I didn't need a business loan, and I used my marketing skills. I also had to promise the previous owners to keep the ridiculous name when they retired. *C'est la vie,*" I explain proudly, and it seems to make him smile. I take a sip of my drink.

"And how does Nate play into this?" he asks with a hint of jealousy as he drinks from his glass.

A laugh escapes me. "I was helping him with his marketing the other day and he also helps me with stuff for my business. Purely business." I keep my face neutral but take quite a bit of pleasure in this.

Jake raises an eyebrow, which makes me sense he doesn't like it too much.

"But anyways, the previous owners still stop by and love testing the changes I've made. We're only open during the day, so we don't have to worry about a dinner rush."

"I'm happy for you, I really am. The place looks great. I feel bad I haven't come in so often lately. But now that I have tried the carrot cake, you've found yourself a repeat customer." He nudges my arm playfully with his and a buzz shoots through me.

"We like repeat customers," I nudge back.

"Even if it's me?"

He is flirting for sure.

"Yeah, especially if it's you." I surprise myself by saying that, and now I am the one who is guilty of flirting, but my stomach spirals from warmth. He seems glad by that remark. "And thanks. But now I'm trying to figure out a blueberry muffin recipe," I add.

"Are you visiting every bakery in a 50-mile radius then?" he jokes.

I point a finger at him. "Hey! You agreed to take me to every bakery within a 10-mile radius of your place to perfect my carrot cake recipe."

"Yeah, but it was okay because we were burning off all those calories," he teases, and I can't help but let my tongue roll to the corner of my mouth, letting my cheeks burn.

"Yeah. Yeah, we were." It comes out soft and maybe he catches that I am reminiscing.

There is a pause as we both get a little lost in old times.

"The Blackhawks won the Stanley Cup after you left." He's trying to break the silence.

I go along with it and point to myself. "Are you saying I was the magic charm?"

"Yeah, because you wore my Blackhawks shirt, I think so. I may need you to wear my Broncos shirt for luck next." He has a glint in his eye while taking a sip from his whiskey, and it's only then that I realize his arm had found a way around my shoulder.

I didn't notice because it was meant to be there. Or at least it feels that way.

"And how would I get into your shirt?" I surprise even myself by how sexy that comes out, and how there is a mischievous grin slapped across my face. The look on his face tells me he enjoys this.

He doesn't miss a beat, "Probably involves my new bed that nobody else has been in." His look is equally serious and entertained.

"Oh, here comes the waiter. Could be my chance to ask for the bill and escape." I give Jake a side glance of mischief.

Jake laughs, "The escape, will you take it?" His eyes hold me in a gaze, and he moves his arm away from me. His face is neutral, but I saw the glimmer in his eyes of hope.

But I don't have a second thought and I look at him with ease. "You know what? I think I will order another drink." I smile, and without thought, I take his arm and drape it back around my shoulder. It makes him smile as he slides a little bit closer to me.

The waiter comes and we order. I order a tonic water to keep my mind clear.

Changing the topic, I decide to bring us back to a neutral zone. "Do you still have eclectic music tastes? I remember how hard it was for you when Dashboard Confessional went on a break," I mock him about the band that he listened to in college and still occasionally listened to when he was preparing for court back in Chicago.

"Hey, off-key acoustic ballads help me get into my concentration zone. Remember Lallapaloosa?"

"That was good. So many good bands in one weekend and the city was insane."

He cracks a look of pride. "The cab ride back?"

I roll my head in delight. "The driver was going to kill us. You had no restraint. I lost three buttons in that cab!" And all we did was make out like two teenagers.

"And I made it up to you." His face has a coy look like he's a good guy. And he is. He made me come in record time when we got back to his place, and the next day, he bought me a new dress with matching lingerie.

I nod slowly in agreement with a soft grin. "You did."

There is a pause, but a good one. Looking at each other, we realize we sailed off-track again. This time we smile, because it just comes naturally, our effortlessness to flirt, be honest, pick up like we were before our world combusted into pieces.

"This is easier than I thought it would be," I admit. He looks at me. "Us talking, I mean. And I enjoy it. We've both had a lot of changes in our lives, but still, that ease is like it never stopped," I reflect softly.

He bites his bottom lip in pleasure and his eyes go light. "Good. And I really enjoy talking to you again too."

These words are the words of my dreams. The icing to my cakes. The chocolate to my brownies.

My lips tug. "We were intense together. Uncontrollable." I can't help but let a half-smile form on my mouth as I look off into the distance.

"We couldn't get enough of each other," he adds as his thumb caresses my cheek.

"Intense in every good and sad way possible," I say distantly. His fingers guide my face with glazed eyes to his direction.

Our eyes meet, my hand covers his hand on my face, and we get lost in our stare. In fact, the room stops as we both look at each other.

Getting re-associated, looking for answers, remembering, maybe hoping. Doing it all without saying a word. Our foreheads touch and our lips don't meet, but I feel them.

"I should probably go," I say softly.

"I don't think you want to," he informs me.

A sound escapes me. "No, I don't. But we both know it's the smart thing to do."

I think I could stay with him all night, but I have no control when I'm around him. He's close to me, and the last hour just showed me that I only want him closer.

Pulling away, I create space. He nods slowly and offers to walk me to my car since we both parked near the hotel. He pays the bill, and we make small talk as we walk. When we reach my car, we stop and stare at each other. There is silence, especially as nobody else seems to be around on this weeknight.

"It's cold out tonight," he comments as he tightens the scarf around my neck. My hand reaches to stop him, but he keeps his hand on me. Our eyes meet.

"You know, I've actually never seen you in winter clothing."

I take a moment to think. "True. We were together in the summer."

"It's way too many layers on you," he smirks, and I can't help but crack a grin.

He brings a hand to each one of my shoulders. "When am I seeing you again, Avery? Dinner? Tomorrow? Because you and I both know this isn't how we should be ending tonight."

"Whoa, someone is smooth," I gently tease him.

"Then say yes to anything. Tonight, dinner, tell me," he counters.

I can't answer. Partly because I really want to say yes, but the other part knows I have the potential to hurt him again.

Still, my filter fails. "Shall we meet Sunday afternoon at your place?" It comes out more eager than I intended, which makes him smirk. "I mean, we could go for a walk or something..." Almost better, but not quite.

"A walk? In the middle of winter?" He grins, knowing very well that I am trying to avoid private settings with him.

"Yeah. A public salted walking path with lots of people sounds reasonable," I explain one-toned with a funny look.

"Okay, a walking path with a lot of people it is."

I nod and move to get in my car, but I stop and turn to him one last time, an electrical zap running through me. Our eyes never parting.

"Night, Jake. Sunday, okay?"

It could mean so many things.

CHAPTER TEN

AVERY

THERE IS A GREAT TRAIL OUTSIDE OF SAGE CREEK, NOT too busy and perfect for this time of year, even when there is a thin layer of snow. We agreed to meet at Jake's place and go with one car as parking can be crazy on the weekends.

He heads out to the driveway of his modern house—not a mansion, but most definitely big enough for a family of five with three cars. He looks good in dark jeans and a dark red Henley shirt that I catch a glimpse of as he zips his coat, a look that I would assume not many people see as he still seems to enjoy his suits on a daily basis. It just makes him even more irresistible.

"Hey," I smile as I kick a pebble on the salted ground, my hands staying in my pockets.

"Hi." He gives me a quick side hug that already has me weakening in the knees.

There's a pause, yet it's not awkward.

"So, shall we do this walk or just stand on my driveway? Either way, I'm good," he cracks out, and a dimple appears.

I smile and we are about to go to his car, but my hand

reaches to the sky. "I think it's going to snow or rain," I mention as I feel a few droplets of sleet falling.

Grabbing his phone, he pulls up a weather app on his screen. "I guess so." He shows me the screen and I bite my lip.

"As much as I love rain, it's cold rain," I admit, which equates to no walk.

"We can grab a drink inside if you want? I swear I won't restrain you with my tie again." He gives me a persuading grin and I can't help but look away, satisfied and letting my tongue circle my mouth. *Oh, that time with the tie.*

"It's okay; you're not wearing a tie today anyways." I give him a playful look.

His arm goes out to lead the way and I follow. He walks in front of me through the garage, inside to the open kitchen, and I take in the surroundings.

"It's a really nice place. Love the exposed brick wall, high ceilings, and the industrial fixtures. Missing a cookie jar and a few plants, but we know your feelings on that," I compliment and tease at the same time.

Jake is standing not far from me, leaning against the counter, and I already feel like he's consuming my air.

"Thanks. I would give you the full tour, but that would mean going upstairs to my bedroom." He offers me his best neutral face, but there is certainly a grin he is trying to hide.

And I am positive my face shows that I enjoyed that comment.

"It's okay, I was fantasizing on giving your granite counter a run for its money anyhow," I refute with a wicked grin, and this time he is the one enjoying my remark.

"It's quartz, actually. And unfortunately for me, that sounded like it was dripping with sarcasm."

"Yeah, it was." *I don't think it was.*

There is a long pause as I study him and recall all the thoughts and memories I've had of him in the last few days.

My mind decides to speak without a filter. "So, can I ask something?"

Jakes looks at me, intrigued. "Anything."

I stare at my fingers gliding along the counter and try to avoid his gaze. "I was just... wondering... the video." I stagger out the words and my eyes glance to meet his own. "You still have it?" I can't help smiling at myself, amused.

A stunted laugh escapes him as his eyes go wide. "And if I said yes? I only ever did that with you."

I don't know what to say, because I'm not sure why I asked other than curiosity. "Me too."

He moves closer to me with his hand cupping my cheek, his mouth leaning into my hair, equally tempting and respectable. We've never been good at keeping our hands off one another, our interaction with each other has always worked on a physical level.

But still, thank goodness I have the sink to support me; I'm not sure I can stand.

Our eyes meet and something in us resonates.

It escalates.

"Tell me what else you remember," he whispers as his hands glide through my hair, tugging slightly.

My eyes search his face and I debate which route to go down, but when his eyes blaze with want, I instantly fall to his ability to lead us down a path that is hazardous in this moment, but too enticing.

Too tempting.

Technically we aren't crossing lines, we're just reminiscing.

"Everything with you. Every time with you," I barely manage to whisper as my body sinks into a floating feeling.

The corners of his mouth slant up in pleasure as his hand reaches to the back of my neck. "Tell me a time, Avery," his voice instructs and churns with desire. Most of all, he is daring me.

So, it is *this* memory lane that we are going down.

Any molecule of resisting this path has been lost. There are two traitors in my body, and they are called my body and mind. They've both surrendered.

"That night on your dining table," I recall with a hint of delight in my voice, my hands cupping his face.

A small laugh escapes him. "Of all our times, you start there?"

It makes me laugh, "We *are* in a kitchen."

He grins at my logic. "The moment you came through the door, I ordered you to take everything off, but the black high heels. I demanded you lay on the dining table with your legs wide open so I could take you, and I did with my mouth because you tasted so damn good, and I bet now you taste just as good." He has a devilish grin on his face and his eyes search me as if he's surveying how he is going to have me.

My eyes roll back in my head and my face dances in his hands as I am reliving the memory, as my internal walls between my legs pulse and spill.

"I screamed your name so loud." I'm proud, almost.

He presses my body to his and I can feel he is swelling.

He hums in the back of his throat, letting his thumb circle my lips, his nose nuzzling my neck and that damn grin getting more smoldering.

Jake's head barely pulls away and his eyes do not leave the sight of my mouth. I cannot help myself and I look to see his erection. I lick my lips in pleasure as his finger hooks under my chin to force me to look back to his eyes.

"You are still so beautiful," he whispers, leaning in towards my ear. My mouth nuzzles into his neck as his arm wraps tightly around my middle and he pulls my body closer.

"What are we doing these last few days?" he asks. "You and I do not dance around each other, Avery. We go right at it from the beginning." He is warning me.

I inhale his scent, wanting so desperately for my leg to wrap around his waist and for him to take me now, any way he pleases.

This is not what I came for. Or is it? I should throw in a disclaimer.

"Jake," it comes out as a pleasured moan. It should have been my warning.

But I don't want to warn him. Or think. Or talk... and we should talk. But in this moment...

Something between us snaps.

JAKE

I am completely aware that Avery's breathing has picked up in anticipation, and when she looks at my mouth, it sends a signal to my brain to turn off and let my cock do the thinking.

My hand wraps around her waist, pulling her against me, as my other hand grasps the back of her head and my mouth captures her bottom lip. It happens fast. A rush.

For a few seconds it is a gentle reunion, but the slow pace doesn't last long. Our mouths devour one another, hungry and hard. She doesn't pull away, I don't pull away, and in this flurry, neither of us knows who is deepening our kiss more.

We both drag our lips apart gently so we can kiss softer to really feel how each other's lips taste and feel after all this time. It is just as good as I remember, better. A perfect fit.

Brushing our lips along one another's, we dive into a hungry kiss again, a sensory overload of epic proportions exploding between us.

I don't think I'm able to get enough of her. No, I know I *cannot* get enough of her.

I've missed her; I've been dreaming of this.

Her arm loops around my neck and her leg wraps around my waist. I lift her to the edge of the counter and my fingers catch one of her wrists, bringing it above her head to place it against the kitchen cupboard. Her leg wraps tighter around my waist, and my cock can feel how much she wants me, even though we have clothing layers between us. Letting my body rock into her, she meets me as her pelvis tilts.

"How have we managed to keep our hands off each other the whole week?" she questions breathlessly, as her mouth explores my neck.

In between my frantic kissing, I tell her against her mouth, "I don't know, but that is changing now."

There are moans escaping even though our lips do not part, I cannot even tell if it is her or me or both. All I know is that this is the only music I want to hear today.

My mouth does not want to leave hers, but I need to taste her neck and I want some of her skin between my teeth. And her breasts, I need one in my mouth too. I am exploring her with abandon in our craze, and I manage to get her fleece zipper undone. She has a cotton blouse with buttons on underneath, and I manage to break a few free.

All the while, she tugs my shirt and manages to get it up enough that our mouths only need to part for a short second so I can get it off. She gapes at my chest for a second and gives me a look of approval, which I will have to tease her about later. Now, I just need more of her.

My mouth drags down her neck to the bare skin on her collarbone and my hand palms one of her fabric-covered breasts, yet I can feel the hardness of her nipple poking through. A moan escapes her as her head falls back. Taking advantage of her open neck, I kiss her throat before finding her lips again.

Her hands reach for my belt and the zipper of my jeans; quickly, I grab her hand and guide her down faster. I am straining for her, and when she touches my covered cock, I do not want to wait. I need to finally be in her again—a sort of homecoming.

A sentiment she confirms. "I-I want you inside me... please," she begs with a raspy voice.

"I want that too, but I need to do it hard," I warn her, and a wave of satisfaction crosses her face before her lips combust onto mine again.

I should lean her back and let my mouth dive between her legs to taste her. But we've both been waiting a long time for this. *Too long.*

My fingers find the waistband of her leggings and I quickly pull them down, and her legs kick them off. Finding underwear, I bring the fabric to the side. *She's in satin.* I let my fingers slide up and down her slit to feel how much she wants me in this very moment, my fingers getting covered in her arousal. She murmurs into my neck, and it is the sound of heaven.

"You are so wet for me. You still feel *so good*, Ave—so

good." I groan as I slip my finger inside her to feel where I need to go, and it is the only destination I ever want.

"Wet only for you. Always for you," she pants. "Please, now," she pleads again as her hand tightens over my boxer briefs.

I'm not religious, but I owe someone a Hail Mary because I manage to grab a condom from my wallet in record time. As I am ripping the condom wrapper open with my teeth, I get a glimpse of Avery with her hair wild across her pink flushed face and her swollen lips. She is breathless from our intensity, and I am confident her watching me open the condom made her even wetter.

But when our eyes meet, a thought crosses my mind, and it stops me in my tracks.

The last time we were intimate was five years ago, in pure bliss when she was...

we were...

...and fuck my morals.

I'm putting on the brakes.

In that very moment, Avery uses that second of pause to also let her brain catch up and take in what we are about to do. Maybe she figures out where my mind went. I don't know.

We pull away from one another, looking at each other with heaving breaths and our foreheads touching, her arms still looped around my neck. She strokes my face with the back of her hand, and I grab her hand and kiss her palm. Letting my fingers then reach for her cheek to rub with my fingers.

"Ave, we should tal—"

Her finger shushes my lips. "I know, Jake. I know," she whispers.

We both wanted to go down this route, but we are both too wise to think we can do this.

It takes a minute, but I bring her back down to earth by helping her back to standing.

Throwing the unused condom to the side, I fasten my pants then let a hand drag through my hair, along with a deep sigh. We both slide down to the floor. Sitting on the tiles and leaning against the cupboards, we recover from our escalation on my kitchen counter.

Avery begins to thread the top buttons of her lacy black top that should be banned for what it does to me.

"Don't do that," I plead with a hitched voice.

A half-smile appears on her face. "You're in luck. I can't. It seems you broke the buttons."

It makes me chuckle slightly with pride.

"Jake, please, for my sanity, throw that shirt back on," she implores with a tight-lipped smile as she tosses me my shirt that found its way to the floor. I smile to myself and oblige, pulling the shirt over my head.

"This probably was *not* a great idea," she comments.

"Not a *bad* idea either."

"I guess not terrible," she adds.

"Definitely not horrible."

"More than okay?" she questions herself. My hand touches her thigh as she speaks. "We took a detour. Maybe we should forget this?"

I can't figure out her tone, but she is nibbling her lip. She seems unsure.

"Maybe," I tilt my head to the side, but then smile to myself. "Nah, I'm not going to."

We look at one another and both have a wry smile.

"This was inevitable," I say.

A deep sigh escapes her. "I know."

We take another moment to allow what is happening between us to sink in. To register what is shifting.

"Almost-sex with your ex on your kitchen counter. I'm hoping that you haven't had to use that sentence before." She offers me a funny look.

I have to shake my head softly with her humor. But then I need to clarify. "You are more than an ex, you know that."

It's why I stopped us.

It catches her off guard. I hope she understands what I mean. She grabs my arm with my watch, and she brings my inner wrist to her lips. It is her way of telling me she understands. Yet, I still wonder what I am to her.

After placing a gentle kiss, she holds my wrist a few extra moments before releasing it.

"I should go."

"Don't do that either. What about that drink?"

She tilts her head side to side. "That's not always innocent with you, but sure."

We slowly drag our bodies off the floor and our eyes hold each other's gaze. My eyes do not leave her as I grab two mugs. Her face tells me she is slightly humored by this whole situation, which is a good thing, as I don't need her to have a reason to avoid me.

Admittedly, I fucked up a little. I took things a step too far there. I had to take us down *that* memory lane, because a voice in me could not resist knowing if she still thinks about us or remembers.

It was not my greatest of moves. Yet, I do not regret it.

After that summer, I tried hard to forget her. But the women I tried hard with; the voltage level was just too low compared to the electricity that I shared with Avery. None of them could give that surge of lust that I had with her and I still have with her.

That connection.

Something tells me our conversation is finally going to go to the place that we have been avoiding, and I need to be the guy she can depend on. No matter how this goes, I have to be the stronger one in this situation. At least if we really are going to have this talk. No tricks or sidetracks.

I walk to her and hand her a mug as she looks out my back sliding door.

"It's really beautiful here," she comments as she admires the forest behind my house.

"Definitely different to the city, that's for sure. We will have to walk the trail another time. It is great. I do trail runs there with Nate or I meet Leo or Lucas with their kids."

"Makes sense. Even when you work a lot, you make time for people. That I know."

"True. And if I recall, making time for you was well worth it," I confess as I lean against the glass door.

She looks at me. "We had a lot of good times," she reflects. She hits me playfully. "We were good together in the bedroom," she admits with her eyes roaming me. Perhaps too suggestively. She walks to the couch and I follow.

"And the kitchen counter, the living room floor, the hallway wall, the elevator, the shower..." I list, and she giggles.

I add as we both sit down, "Mastered the art of lying in bed and talking too."

Her face turns slightly elated. "Yeah. Yeah, we did." She bites her lip. "We didn't end because we weren't good together."

Our bodies move closer to one another, like they are two puzzle pieces meant to fit.

"I know. It was just timing and life throwing us a curve-ball as the reason we ended," I explain. She nods.

And before we get more comfortable on the couch, I need to ask. "Want something stronger?" I offer. I sure as hell need it.

"Yes." It comes out neutral.

I go to the kitchen to find wine and glasses. It's an open-plan living area, so I show her a bottle of white and she gives me an agreeing look. Quickly, I make my way back to her.

"Your kitchen looks like it's a dream for cooking," she admires as she takes her wine glass from my hand.

"I don't really use the kitchen much. Mostly order in."

She offers a warm smile. "Sounds like the typical bachelor life. What do you order?"

"The Chinese restaurant knows me by first name, fairly positive the Thai one too. That one place you loved in the city actually delivers next day here via a special ice box or something. Haven't tried it yet though."

"The one with the hot dogs and Italian subs? Uh, those were *so* good," she reminisces.

"Yeah. We should try one day. I remember how much you loved the hot dogs but couldn't stand the smell when you were pre—" I stop mid-sentence and realize what I was just about to say. My eyes slowly close then reopen as her face fades to neutral.

And just like that, there we are.

The conversation we were waiting for.

We both lean against the back of the brown leather sofa with wine in hand, and our faces turn to one another.

Avery lets out a breath. "You mean when I was pregnant?"

It isn't a question; it's a fact, and I nod softly.

"It's okay, we can't tiptoe around it forever. It's what we

were going to talk about anyways, right?" She looks at me blankly.

Taking her glass out of her hand, I place it with mine on the coffee table. Immediately pulling her to me and wrapping my arms around her.

Avery isn't just an ex; she is the one who I share the biggest connection in life with.

CHAPTER ELEVEN

JAKE

SEEING HER AGAIN AND IT'S AS CLEAR AS DAY, THAT summer.

She had texted me that she needed me to come back to my apartment right away. It was the middle of the day and I needed to be at the office as I had just landed my biggest client up to that point of my career.

But somehow, I knew I needed to go home. It felt urgent. I casually walked into my kitchen, asking her what couldn't wait, and I stopped mid-sentence when I saw Avery distraught. My eyes looked to what her eyes were fixated on, and there was a row of tests on the counter. All positive.

Suddenly, we were two people who had to put their lust on the backburner, because we had an unexpected predicament and every brain cell in our heads was laser focused on every decision. Looking back, it shouldn't have been such a surprise; for being two smart people, we weren't that careful.

But it's that one memory that gets to me every time. A glimpse of what could have been.

Sitting on the edge of my bed, I loosen my tie and begin to unbutton my sleeves, admiring the latest ultrasound photo on my dresser.

This wasn't planned, and it wasn't until we heard the heartbeat that it hit us—we are going to do this.

My eyes turn to Avery who stands in my doorway. She just got back from work and basically almost lives here. Even I know those tight pencil skirts are on their final days as she wears a blouse to cover her stomach. Avery has not been able to stomach much lately and has been doing her best to hide it at work. I get it. I work in corporate law and see enough cases where pregnancy of an employee played a role. The world has strides to make.

I wave my hands to indicate for her to come to me. When she is within distance, I grab her hand to hold and wheel her around, so she's sitting on my lap. Her arms wrap around my neck.

"Everything okay?" I mumble as I kiss her shoulder.

She kisses my cheek. "Yeah, only a little dizzy today." Immediately, I'm on full alert and adjust my body so I can look at her. Study her. Examine her.

"Do you want me to get you something? You took the vitamins?" I begin, and she has to laugh.

"Relax, Counselor, yes, taking the vitamins, eating well, sleeping more, and we are having only gentle sex, per your insistence," Avery assures me with a smile. "It will be fine."

"I know it took you awhile to adjust to this news, I mean, it wasn't exactly planned. But we will make it work. You can move in here; we will live here or find a place—"

"Jake. I love your positivity, but it's also okay to acknowledge that this really wasn't planned, like, at all, and if it hadn't happened, then we wouldn't be moving in together now," she admits but with ease. Because it's true. It was only supposed to be the summer. In fact, her time in Chicago was supposed to end next week as her project finishes. Long-distance would have been near impossible for us due to our work schedules, and unless I pass the California bar, then my work remains in Chicago.

Cradling her head with my hands to ensure she looks at me, my grin gives her a warning. "Avery. Does it look like I am complaining about this unexpected turn of events?" I raise my eyebrows and graze her cheek and neck with my lips. She shakes her head no. "Come away with me. Next weekend, before we start to tell everyone we're together, let alone having a baby, let's head up to Wisconsin for the week-end." The way I say it hopefully sends excitement through her, and my eyes are inviting and warm, because we need to talk about us, and I want to surprise her.

She nods her head yes with a sparkle in her eye.

"You're in the middle of your biggest case yet, and you want to go away for the weekend? What have I done to you?" she teases me.

Kissing her neck, I tell her, "A lot, you have done a lot to me."

"Mmm, sounds like you're getting frisky. Let me take a shower, okay?"

I nod. "Sure, I'll join you in a sec." I reluctantly let her move off me and watch her walk away.

When she's out of sight, I walk to my dresser drawer, pull it open, and look at the small black box with a ring inside before setting it back in my drawer in a place I know Avery won't find it. She will see it this weekend when we go away because I plan to tell her I love her and want her to be my wife.

I should have already told her, but our heads have been everywhere, and I don't want her to feel like I'm asking her *just because she's pregnant. She deserves a romantic gesture, because she is everything that I didn't know I was looking for.*

Smiling to myself, I continue to take off my shirt and throw it to the other side of the room. But as I walk towards the bathroom, I already sense something is different.

Avery

I've been avoiding this exact conversation all week—well, five years, really. But I knew it was our eventual topic of discussion at some point. Just didn't think post-almost-sex was going to be the way to get us there. But you know, that's okay, because it makes this slightly more comfortable.

This talk. I owe it to him. I owe it to myself.

I interlace our arms as we look forward. I need to begin somewhere.

"It's why you stopped, isn't it? In the kitchen, I mean. You remembered the last time we were together like that was when I was pregnant."

A deep sigh escapes him.

"Yeah," he replies, and it's simple. His face turns serious. "Just... we should talk about it. You haven't mentioned it once yet."

"Why haven't you brought it up?"

He ponders how to explain. "I was waiting. I felt it had to come from you. I don't know how you coped with it in the end and I didn't want to pressure you to talk about it."

Looking at him, I don't know what to say.

I sigh. "We met in May, by July we knew we were already pregnant, and by the beginning of September, it was all over. We were unexpectedly going to be parents together, but life had other plans for us, for him." Jake grabs my hands to hold and kisses my palm as he interlaces our fingers.

I continue. "Everyone handles it differently. Views it differently. Nobody knows except you, and maybe that's why when I saw you, my head went into an immediate spin, because there you were, and with you, I can be open about it. I'm not used to that."

"I already guessed that, doesn't take a psychologist to figure it out. And I didn't tell anyone either." After a prolonged pause, he asks, "How do you view it?"

I consider what to say and bite my lip as I collect my thoughts. Tears well in my eyes, but then I say honestly, "As a beautiful surprise that wasn't meant to be."

Jake kisses the top of my head and lets his fingers stroke my hair.

"I think so too," he whispers. We let our statements sink in for a minute. "And how did you cope with it?"

"Well, I didn't at first. I mean, I ran away from you; doesn't that say enough?" I look at him. "But I buried myself in work, went to a yoga healing retreat that was borderline cultish and most definitely failed on the healing front. Baked *a lot* more. Actually, maybe it gave me the drive to bake more. It's maybe ironic, I used your legal advice of how to negotiate a deal when I left the agency. Like we talked about when I was pregnant, since we knew I was going to have to leave the agency to move to Chicago permanently. Well, I used that advice to help me leave, and now I am here where you are."

A look that I can't figure out overcomes him. Sadness or contentment.

"I worked a lot too," he admits softly, "put everything

into that case and won big. But I moved here because being in Chicago just reminded me too much of, well..."

Now I return a look similar to what he gave me a few moments before.

"Do you ever think about what life would be like if it hadn't happened?" I lean my head against his shoulder as I look forward.

Jake leans back on the sofa and his thumb rubs his upper lip. "Sometimes. I tucked it in the back of my head, what happened. I think about what life would be like now if he was born... our last five years would have looked different, that's for sure. Seeing you again definitely puts it all in the front of my head again," Jake confesses in a neutral tone, as if he has stripped all emotion from the memory.

There's a pause.

"I think about it more than I should," I explain. "What our life would have looked like, I mean..." I can't finish, as another tear falls.

He holds me closer as we soak in a minute of quiet. I try to picture what must be in his head. It maybe aligns with my thoughts. Before I think of the life we could have built, I snap back to the present.

"I'm sorry I didn't handle it well," I acknowledge. I said nothing for days, yet Jake held me endlessly. When we got the news, we both had tears. Based on blood work, we learned he was a boy. There was no explanation of why, other than it felt unfair; at 14 weeks, we should have been in the clear. Jake, after a minute, shook himself out of it, and like a light switch, he put on a strong demeanor to take care of me. He remained controlled and did his best to support me.

My withdrawal created distance between us, until a

week later when he begged me to stay. *"I want you to stay. We can take time, anything. Just —just stay..."*

But I chose to leave.

"Jake, I can't stay. It's too painful. Too many reminders." The words still seethe with pain when I remember how we were an intertwined mess of tears and emotion standing in his kitchen. *"We don't have to be together because of a baby now. You're off the hook. I'm not your responsibility anymore. I need to figure this out on my own. Jake, you deserve everything that will make you happy, but right now, we only remind each other of what we lost."*

He reluctantly let me pull away before I kissed his inner wrist as a form of goodbye.

And that was that.

He drapes an arm around my shoulder, bringing me to lean against him and letting me continue.

"For months I was lost. I could think of a hundred reasons why losing him was my fault." Tears form and are on the verge of falling. He adjusts his position, and his hands cup my face forcefully, so I have no choice but to look at him.

"Hey. It is not your fault. It's no one's fault," he assures me firmly.

"It took me awhile, but I do accept it now."

"We will never know why it happened, but one day, you will maybe have another baby, and fate just gave you a different timeline." Jakes says this with a kindness and vulnerability that I recognize. I want to tell him that I struggle seeing myself having a baby with anyone else. Not since I envisioned having our baby together. But maybe that is too much.

"Maybe..."

The sound of the rain outside fills the room.

My free hand grabs my wine glass and I take a sip to calm my nerves. Jake follows suit. After, we both set our glasses down and we look at each other. Because we know this is not going to get easier.

He pulls me to his chest as he leans back on the sofa, taking me with him. We both breathe and take in the silence.

"You shouldn't have left. I was hurting too," he states, yet continues to hold me close and stroke my hair with his fingers.

"I was hurting for a long time, but it was also worse because I didn't have you near. You must be so angry at me for leaving like that." I state, pushing softly against his chest and moving away so I can see his face.

He bites his lip and rubs the back of his head.

"I was—it felt like a knife ripped through me. Sometimes, I still want to be angry. You took away our chance of being together. You could have stayed, and we would have tried being together for the long haul. But I knew how traumatic it was for you, it was your body that went through it. I had the shitty ringside seat. I figured I was just too much of a reminder for you."

My throat aches from how honest he is being, how understanding. "And now?"

"This conversation is maybe the closure we needed about the baby. We finally have it." He touches my cheek with his thumb and lets his eyes look deeply into mine. Then he pulls me back to his chest.

There is a silence between us, yet it feels comforting. I let out a deep exhale.

"I was going to reach out to you when I was ready." My throat feels like it's cracking, and a pain in my heart is discouraging another truth that I need to tell him.

"Why didn't you reach out?" he asks, one-toned.

"Guilt, mostly... I walked away. But then a year later..." It reluctantly comes out of my mouth and I look away from his gaze.

"Avery, what happened a year later?" His tone is stern.

Sighing, I get up off the sofa and walk to the window where I cross my arms and look out. "For some reason, I decided to look you up online, even though I knew your contact details. But I needed a clue where you were in your life..."

I feel his eyes on me. "And?"

"I saw an article on you about a case you won and there was photo of you with a woman. I just assumed..."

Glancing behind my shoulder, I see Jake's eyes darkening and his nostrils almost flaring.

I continue on, "I was scared I would mess up your life if I reached out. You were on the high track career-wise when I left. I thought with time you'd found someone. I didn't want to ruin that for you. Maybe I was a reminder for you of what we lost, or you couldn't get past the fact I left. I didn't reach out, and I regret that."

He lets out a bitter laugh to himself and rubs a hand across his face. "Avery, there was nobody. My guess is you saw the photo of me and one of the long-standing partners' daughter's. Nothing happened."

We stare at one another as we take in all the facts about our post-us life. I return to sitting on the couch.

He speaks first. "I phoned your brother two months after you left."

I'm taken aback by his statement. He continues, "I didn't know what you did or did not tell him about us, so I casually asked how you were. He said you seemed different and couldn't figure out why. I wanted to get on the first flight to you, but I didn't want you to hurt more by seeing me, because you had begged me to leave you alone when you left."

My throat cracks from the fact that we both wanted to reach out.

He touches my shoulder and I glance down at his hand. "But if you had contacted me, then yeah, I would have rushed at the chance to see you. Becoming named partner at the firm went to the bottom of my priority pile after that summer, and finding someone else was just fucking impossible. It's different for me, maybe because I don't have the same physical connection to the miscarriage? Sure, seeing you makes me think of the baby, but mostly I think of everything else with you... the fun and amazing things with you."

We both look at each other, realizing we both have misgivings about the fallout, yet we find a comfortable embrace. This is the way it should have been all those years ago. Coping together, holding each other, never letting go. I fit in his hold, I feel at ease in his arms, and he belongs in my life, always has. We sit there for what seems like ages.

My fingers place lazy designs over his chest, and I breathe in the feeling of his arms wrapped around me, smelling his scent and taking notice of the way his chest moves.

Letting memories of him float in and out of my head, as new possibilities appear scattered in my thoughts. He must feel this too.

Relief. Peace. Hope.

After a while, I go to the bathroom and clear up my raccoon eyes and return to the living room, where we finish our much-needed wine in one gulp and set the glasses on the kitchen counter.

Yet still, I feel numb, and maybe he feels it too. Our

conversation affected us. I return to the living room and I just fall into his comforting embrace again as we sprawl out on the sofa.

"Well, that was an upbeat conversation." I'm 100% sarcastic, which Jake appreciates.

"Do you want something to eat? It's past dinner time," Jake offers, but I shake my head no. "What time is it?" I ask, grabbing his wrist with his grandfather's watch, letting my finger brush the glass of the watch face.

"Almost eight."

"I forget how I lose track of time when I'm with you." I try to crack a smile.

It's true. We met at three for a walk, and now here we are.

I smile softly. "Thankfully, I'm off tomorrow. I think I may need it after this afternoon."

"Lucky. I have to be in court by ten. But I feel better now that we've had this conversation. My emotions may still be a little thrown, but it feels right that we spoke about it. We still have a lot to talk about when it comes to us." He's candid and that awes me.

Us. That label floats around me with promise. My head locks in on that word.

There is a pause and I hesitate, but decide to just ask.

"Do you think I can stay here tonight? Just to sleep," I ask gently and clarify what I mean as he continues to stroke my hair as I lean against his chest.

He kisses the top of my head. "Yeah, absolutely. I can grab some sheets for the spare room."

My head peers up. Shaking my head gently no.

"I don't want to be alone, and your arms feel right. Can we just sleep?" I request and explain.

His face has a grin that quickly widens with a short

chortle escaping him. He gives me a warm knowing look. "Did you really think I was going to let you sleep in the guest room? Not a fucking chance."

It makes me smile and my cheek muscles tighten with joy.

"Oh? The coveted new bed that no other woman has seen?" I tease and wiggle my eyebrows as I get up and off the couch.

I could have sworn he mumbled *you're the only woman who will ever see it,* but I'm not sure if my ears are playing tricks. "What was that?" I tilt my head to the side.

A look of fun spreads across his face, "Get upstairs, Avery," he orders and scoots me forward.

"Bossy."

A few minutes later, I wait for him as I lie in the middle of the bed on top of the covers, wearing nothing but a t-shirt he gave me to wear, and it most definitely doesn't cover my legs. A week ago, I maybe would have been nervous with a thin wall around me. Now, this feels comfortable, easy, and my heart races. I do not need walls; I can be myself.

He emerges from the bathroom wearing sweatpants and no shirt. I swallow and maybe even curse under my breath. His perfectly defined body and muscles seem to have developed even more under this light.

He draws in a breath. "I am a good guy tonight," he reminds himself softly through clenched teeth as he looks at me, which makes me smile.

"How do you want me?" I ask, knowing very well that line was sizzling with innuendo, and my voice was a tad on the side of inviting. But I want to make him laugh.

Jake shakes his head with an amused grin and his hand meets his forehead. "Avery, you're killing me here."

"What? I don't remember which side of the bed you

sleep on. It has been a while. Maybe you changed your routine," I shrug, biting my lip.

Jake looks at me, puzzled, and then lets out a small laugh. "Really? It doesn't matter to me," he says as I move, and he throws the covers back so I can crawl in.

I can't seem to take my eyes off of him, and I appear to be the target of his gaze too.

"Do you mind if I sleep just in boxers?" he asks as a true gentleman would, pointing to his sweatpants.

I shake my head no. "After what went down on your kitchen counter, now you want to be polite about removing clothing?" I tease with an entertained look.

"Says the one who unbuckled my belt and begged," he counters.

"Debating with an attorney is pointless," I say with resignation, and give him a look of defeat.

Satisfied, he takes his watch off, setting it on the side table, and throws his sweatpants to the floor before crawling into bed.

Normally, I would give a guy credit for sleeping in a bed half-naked next to a woman. But this isn't like that. We need this contact. This comfort.

We both roll to our sides and look at each other, meeting in the middle of the bed and sharing a pillow even though he has four. His fingers push some strands of my hair behind my ear. When he removes his hand, I stop him and keep his hand on my face by placing my hand on top of his. Our eyes lock with each other. We're enjoying being this close, saying nothing, just listening to the hail against the window.

"Is it crazy that I only now feel like I finally have closure about what happened? As if I could only have it because of you? The missing piece. I've kept it in for so long, as if you are the only one I could share it with," I admit gently.

His fingers clutch my lower jaw, and he props my chin up to ensure our eyes look deeply into each other's.

"Not crazy at all. It's how I feel too."

He kisses my cheek, a long slow lingering kiss, and I do not want his lips to leave. Then he reaches behind him to turn the light off. He returns to the middle of the bed where our arms find each other, and I prop a leg over his hip.

"I don't know what happens now," I whisper in the dark as I nuzzle into his chest.

"Me neither," he confesses softly, and he kisses me on the forehead as I squeeze him tighter.

My head tilts up, and through the small amount of light coming through the drapes, I can see the outline of Jake's face. He looks down at me and very quickly our lips meet for a gentle reconnection. Soft and sweet. We could easily consume each other now, I'm sure, but this is not that kind of night. After holding the kiss for a few seconds, we pull away and fall into an embrace of sleep.

The most comforting night of sleep of my life, feeling safe and cared for, as if no time has passed.

Being with him.

Because he has a piece of me that nobody else ever will, but I'm not sure I know how to handle that, or if I can get past the fact that I walked away. Maybe this is only closure. Not everyone gets that second chance to try again.

But surely this all has to mean something. We must be heading somewhere. Closing one chapter and opening another.

CHAPTER TWELVE

JAKE

WAKING AT SEVEN, MY EYES BLINK A FEW TIMES, AND my arm feels numb. Smiling to myself, I see the evidence in my arms of a surreal night. I have been waiting five years for a glimmer of closure, and last night we had something that felt close.

I never thought I would see Avery again, let alone be able to have an open and raw conversation like that. Sleeping together and holding each other just felt right. The way we needed to end the day.

As I shift slightly, trying not to wake her, her body moves gently as a soft throaty mumble escapes her. Avery's arm tightens around me as she continues to sleep. She looks angelic and like she belongs in my bed.

She really does.

This is the woman who I was going to have forever with. It hurt so much when she walked away, but I understand where her mind was. I always figured it would take her awhile to overcome what happened to her, to us. Now I know it certainly did take time.

Avery wasn't herself when she left me all those years

ago, but now when I see her smiling as she looks at cakes in her bakery... I guess her spark did eventually return in some form. She's in a good place in her life, and I'm happy her decisions led her here to where I am.

By eight, I'm standing in the kitchen drinking a coffee, wondering if I should wake her or let her sleep in as I need to leave by nine. Heading to my room, I lean down and kiss her forehead softly and look at her as she lies there, entangled in the sheets with her legs on display. Her light brown hair is sprawled out on the pillow. My bed will smell of her vanilla scent. She's a beautiful wreck.

Deciding I don't want to wake her as she was sleeping so peacefully, I leave a note and a spare key on the pillow next to her.

Avery,

I didn't want to wake you. I had to get to court, but stay as long as you want. Coffee is in the kitchen. Use the spare key when you leave. Last night needed to happen.

Jake xx

By 12, I'm out of court and look at my phone to see Avery texted me.

Avery: Last night was something, Jake. And I only just woke at 11. I haven't slept that deep or long since Chicago. Thank you xx

I let my thumb slide along my phone screen so I can re-read the message a few times, with a smile forming on my lips.

Me: Anytime. xx

I'm meeting Lucas for lunch and see he's waiting at a table for me. Giving him a nod, I slide into the booth.

"There you are. You went MIA yesterday. Couldn't reach you," Lucas says as he pours soy sauce into a dish.

"Yeah, sorry. Had something going on," I tell him as neutrally as possible.

My phone vibrates.

Avery: By the way, I now have your shirt.

Me: Keep it. You wear it better than me.

Avery: Good answer.

"What are you smiling about? Something to do with Avery? You saw her yesterday, no?" Lucas asks with a piece of sushi in his mouth.

I look up at Lucas who is studying me.

"Oh man, someone is smitten," he teases.

"It isn't like that. *Really*." Because Avery is more than that to me. That thought takes over me and he must pick up on my face change.

"Everything okay?" Lucas raises, concerned.

"It's complicated between Avery and me. But something happened yesterday that we both needed," I begin. "No, we didn't have sex," I clarify. Well, we almost did, but I don't think my friend needs to hear the details of what happened on my expensive counter.

"Okay, go on," Lucas is intrigued.

"When Avery and I were together five years ago, it was only supposed to be a no-strings kind of thing, but it turned to more—a lot more... it just wasn't meant to be." I adjust my shoulder when I say that.

Lucas leans back in his seat and looks at me.

"We needed yesterday for closure. I needed it for closure. Now that we have it, I wonder—no, I *know* there is something else for us," I profess, because I feel that I can look to the future, and I want her to be part of it.

"Sounds like something worth exploring," Lucas encourages. "I'm sure you both changed in the last five years, but I can imagine for the better. Do you still feel something when you're with her?" Lucas asks as he takes a drink from his iced tea.

"Yeah, I do, and I think she does too. It just feels easy between us. Natural. That chemistry is still fire. But how do you pick up after such a long break?"

"One of you takes the lead and then you go for it." Lucas offers a comforting smile and pushes the plate of sushi my way.

Taking the lead is something I can do. I want to do. Now that we got the difficult discussion out of the way, I am not letting Avery walk away. I am determined, and she never could resist that characteristic.

I mean, fuck, I'm almost 35 and drive an Audi SUV. It's time to fill it with a wife and kids, maybe a dog too. Who better than the woman I was going to ask to spend forever with? And seeing her now, I want to ask her again for forever. Granted, I should maybe start with dinner first...

My phone vibrates again.

Avery: And the key? What should I do with it?

She inserts a winking emoji.

Me: Keep that too. Save me if I ever get locked out of my house?

Avery: Sounds reasonable. But risky. You might return to some plants and a goldfish in your living room.

Me: It's a risk I'm willing to take.

"Earth to Jake. Yoo-hoo." Lucas is waving a hand in my face, bringing me back to reality.

"Sorry. I got sidetracked."

"No shit. But I get it. So, what's your move?" Lucas asks, adjusting his shoulders.

I contemplate. "Not sure yet, but she will certainly get a

move from me. Maybe let her relax a little after yesterday. It was a lot. I'll try and see her later this week if she wants it."

"You're a good guy. If I were in your position, I don't think I would have your restraint," Lucas admits.

"Trust me, I wasn't always a good guy." Definitely not. When Avery came into the bar that night in Chicago, I was thinking dirty things. And when she came home with me, I demanded her to do those dirty things, and she obliged.

"That's a true story." Lucas grins, as we got up to some trouble when we were in graduate school together.

"So enough about me. What's up with you?" I ask, trying to divert his attention and grabbing a piece of sushi in the process.

"Theo is visiting next weekend since his mother is off to marry husband number two." Lucas has a slight disdain in his voice as it was a messy divorce with his first wife, and he now sees his son on weekends, but after a moment, a smile forms. "Abby is busy with volunteering at the animal shelter. So please adopt a puppy," His glowing look could be because it's puppies, but my guess is it's for his girlfriend who is a veterinarian.

"For sure, I'll donate to the puppies, but I'm not taking one home," I remind him.

"Actually, Avery donates a lot of baked dog treats to the shelter," Lucas adds.

"Well, then on second thought, I guess will be taking an interest in puppies." I grin as I take a sip of my iced tea.

After lunch, I head back to my office to check in with my secretary and research some cases. By five, I am ready to leave, which is not like me. I struggle not to text Avery. But I am curious if she will take the next step before I get the chance to lead.

Getting home at 8pm is not unusual for me. Not when I am preparing for deposition. After parking my car in the garage, I squint my eyes when I see light coming out from under the door to the kitchen. That's odd. But I mastered Krav Maga and feel confident that I will survive.

As soon as I open the door and see my dining table, my eyes dart to the goldfish in a bowl that is awaiting me. Avery should not have my key. But she *really* should.

Heading to the table, I look at the fish swimming feverishly in the bowl, with a plant and blue castle. Laughing softly to myself, I begin to undo the sleeves on my shirt, and as I turn, I stop dead in my tracks.

"Freddy the fish is allergic to dogs, so I guess you don't need to worry about getting roped into adopting a puppy." Avery has a sly look on her face as she sits on the edge of the sink, wearing white sneakers, a jean jacket, and a long green blouse dress that goes down to just above her knees, *just*. Her hair is in a messy knot on the top of her head. Her look is priceless.

It seems she has been waiting for me. And that thought drips in hope that she has been waiting for me to do everything... to her.

Slowly I glide towards her as I grin, admiring her.

"You would only know about my fear of getting roped into adopting a puppy if you were talking with someone. So, have you been talking about me?" I enquire with a grin.

She realizes she is a little bit caught and her tongue circles inside her mouth as she smiles to herself. I enjoy seeing her squirm.

"Treat Freddy the fish well." She hops off the edge of the sink as if she is going to leave. I step in the way between the sink and the kitchen island. Avery will not be able to escape.

"Have you been waiting long?"

"No. I figured you still worked long days. I warned you that your key isn't safe with me." She looks directly at me and stands tall.

"Quite the opposite. I like this. Even if it means I now have to try and keep a freaking fish alive," I admit.

Realizing that I did not get to finish unbuttoning my cufflinks, I return to that task. But Avery, just like those years ago, takes over. Her hands undo them for me and her then fingers go to the buttons at my collar and loosens those too, her touch sending heat through my veins and a tinge of excitement to my core. By the look on her face, she enjoys this too because her fingers linger a little longer than needed at my collarbone. When she finishes, she takes a step back with a look of fulfilment.

My eyes question her, and I ask, "So, are you staying or going?"

She licks her lips and looks away. "Truthfully, I didn't think past delivering a goldfish and giving you his container of fish food."

Not only is she adorable when she says this, but she means it too.

Stepping closer to her, I place my hands on her hips then give her a lingering kiss on her cheek. I want to taste her mouth, but I'm not sure where we are picking up from the other night.

We're finding our way back to each other, but maybe it's a process.

"I'm sorry for what happened on the kitchen counter yesterday. Actually, not sorry at all. But maybe the timing wasn't right."

A hum escapes her. "I am equally guilty. Pretty positive I guided your hands to where they should go." She's trying to get a rise out of me.

I pull her waist flush to me. "Positive I don't need a guide," I protest.

"Hmm, sounds like a challenge."

"Stay. We can watch a movie or something?" I give her my best grin of innocence. She starts laughing and it fills the room and breaks down my defenses.

"An actual movie or *our* movie." Avery walks past me, throws her coat off, and goes to flop on the sofa.

"All options are on the table, but let me go upstairs and change out of my suit first, unless you want to help with that," I call out as I head towards the stairs.

Turning around briefly, I see she is giving me a wry smile.

Ten minutes later, I come downstairs, changed out of my suit into my sweats and she has mugs of tea on the coffee table. She is battling with the remote.

"Couldn't help noticing you made the bed. Your bed-making skills have improved," I tell her as I sit on the couch.

"Do not even start. It is a serious topic. By the way, I noticed the amazing artwork on your fridge." She indicates with the remote, pointing behind her.

"Oh yeah. That is from my niece. My sister Becca is in the middle of a divorce and it's an ugly one, so I watch my niece, Stella, every now and then."

Her face warms. "That's really sweet. I bet you nail your uncle duties. I remember you always picked out gifts to send to her when she was just born, every time we went someplace cool in the city," she recalls.

"I can be a sweet guy."

"I know. You try and act all hard sometimes, but you can be very nurturing." She may be trying to goad me.

I scratch my cheek, "Nurturing?" I ask, puzzled.

"Yeah. Nurturing, caring. All those warm and fuzzy adjectives that damage your image as a merciless lawyer." Her half-smirk and narrowed eyes tell me she is being honest, yet is also trying to rile me.

She quickly moves us along. "So, we know we're not watching *Suits* as we know your views on that, even though everyone in this town apparently deems you the local Harvey Specter." She drags it out with her lips quirked.

Well, yes, I have strong views on watching a fictional courtroom after being in a real one.

"What about a home makeover show or cooking show? You seem like someone who likes Chip and Joanna?" She taps her finger on her lips as she studies me.

"Is that that couple from Texas that house flips? Yeah, that's a good show," I admit, coming to sit next to her.

"Great. We could settle that one out of court then." She winks and places her legs over my knees as she puts the TV on.

Just like that, I remember how much fun I had with her. Every conversation was easy, every sentence witty, our bodies always hanging off each other.

But I can't look at the television. I can only look at her.

A sexy and sultry look appears on her face. "Thank you for the shirt, I was planning on using it again tonight."

So, this is the path we are going down. I was going to give it to the end of the week—considering the conversation we had yesterday—but I'm happy to see she is at ease again.

"That's all you'd be wearing?" I wonder.

"Who said I would use it for wearing?"

Fuck, she knows she is riling me up. She does it better than anyone else I've been with.

"I'm trying to be a gentleman," I declare as I move closer to her.

"Fair enough. So, what does Jake the gentleman do?" She smirks as her fingers dance on my hand.

I take her hand in mine. "Ask if you want to meet for a coffee in a public place? Go for a drink? Go for a run? Anything but ask what my shirt would be witnessing tonight."

Her eyes meet mine. I want to lean into her to kiss her and I am thinking how incredibly soft and full her lips are and how they dance with mine.

Something tells me she's thinking the same thing as she moves closer to me on the sofa, her eyes staring at my mouth, her teeth biting her bottom lip in anticipation.

"You didn't want to stop yesterday, did you?" I know the answer, but I want to hear it.

"No. I didn't. But it was the right thing to do. You were the good guy."

"And if I'm the bad guy tonight?" I ask as I move in slowly.

"Definitely take me hard like you mentioned. You are *very good* at that."

Her feet reach for my waist and her calves circle around my waist as she pulls me to her with her legs.

My head moves towards her. "Can the bad guy kiss you tonight?"

She pretends to consider with her finger coming to her chin. "A chaste kiss would be okay, I think." Her grin is too sweet for my restraint to handle, the undertone to encourage me too strong.

Our eyes are agreeing.

And we move.

But as we are about to hit a homerun, her phone goes off. My phone goes off. And the mood is broken. The world has other plans for us.

Avery literally huffs in agony as she grabs her phone from her pocket. I grab my phone from the coffee table. I look at her as I listen to my phone, my mind is in a tug-o-war if I should behave or try to take us back on route.

"No, it's okay, man." *It's not,* but Leo has been keeping me busy lately with business and I can't complain. "Yeah, send the contract over and you will have an answer from me tomorrow by 9am... good luck with the screaming toddler I hear in the background. Night, man." I hang up and look at Avery who also just hung up.

"Sorry, that was Abby. I missed her text, so she called. Her dog is sick, and Lucas is heading out of town. She wants me to help her with her dog, which is crazy because she is a vet. But the dog is dead weight, and she needs help getting him in the car." The disappointment in her voice is clear.

I look at her with amusement. "If you wanted to make an excuse to leave, you must have a better one you can come up with, because this story has a lot of holes."

She laughs at me and shows me her phone.

"I have evidence, Mr. Attorney. Exhibit A," she teases as she shows me the photo of a Labrador wrapped in a blanket, and to be honest, he does look like he may be losing a lung.

I hold my hands up. "Okay, seems legit."

I follow her to the kitchen where she grabs her coat and bag. She now seems like she's in a rush on her way to the front door. But she stops quickly and kisses me on the cheek, lingering just a little longer, her hand on my cheek and her thumb rubbing my lips. Then she drags her hand to grab my wrist and brings her lips to my inner wrist for a feathery kiss that makes me smile.

"Next time, okay?" She makes it sound as if our minds were in the same place of where our night was going to go.

Avery smiles, and as she turns, I gently grab her arm and twirl her back to me. In a quick sweep, my head tilts down to her and I let my mouth graze her soft lips. Going side to side, nuzzling and feeling her breath, just enough to touch her and just enough to make her want more. I pull away, letting my knuckles caress up and down her cheek. I give her an innocent smile while thinking not-so-innocent thoughts.

"Look at your moves, Casanova." Avery lets her fingers tap against my chest as she bites her lip in enjoyment. "Goodnight, Jake. I'll see you around."

CHAPTER THIRTEEN

JAKE

THE NEXT DAY, I GO TO VISIT GRAMPS. HE'S LYING IN his bed, his tray table between us with a checkerboard on it. He looks a little weaker than last week. It's his lungs, they say, but he isn't in pain. He still doesn't fail to listen and ask questions.

"Is it serious?"

"Yeah, she just doesn't know it yet. Or maybe she does. She isn't new in my life, but it's been a while since we saw each other," I confess with a confident look.

My grandfather leans back in bed, crossing his arms. "Okay, and why has it been a while?"

Debating what to say, I decide to be open and honest with the man who has played such a vital role in my life.

"We were together in Chicago very briefly," I remind him.

"Why briefly?" The old man won't let me get away with vague details.

I try to brush it off. "It doesn't matter, Gramps."

My grandfather studies me for a good minute and lets

out a sigh before bringing his hand to his chin. "You loved this girl?"

Something resonates. Returning to my grandfather's inquisition, I answer, "A lot."

"She knew this?"

Taking a moment to think about his question, my mind recalls those months. It was supposed to be a no-strings relationship. But very quickly, we both knew that was not for us. We wanted to spend every spare second with each other, make the most of those few months. We cared for each other. I was crazy about her and I told her a lot.

After the baby news, we made plans for raising the baby together. But we didn't talk about getting married or love. We were too preoccupied with the logistics of unexpectedly having a baby. I was saving the "us" conversation for when I asked her to go away with me for the weekend. In fact, even though I knew that Avery was the one I was in love with... I never told her.

I should have told her the other night. I also could have asked her to marry me even after the baby was gone. That is my mistake which I've carried around for five years. My guilt.

She was so open with me the other night, and I should have been too. She should know I also made mistakes. But I didn't tell her because I felt it would make her feel worse for walking away. It didn't seem right or fair.

I shake my head, ashamed in a way. "No. I didn't tell her. I wanted to, but something unexpected kind of detoured all our conversations. I regret it now."

"So, tell her now. You are seeing her, no?" He not only states it, he requests it. I contemplate his words.

"Turns out she moved to Sage Creek, and her friends

are my friends. It's a small world, really. And we're speaking again, reconnecting again."

"That sounds like the universe giving you a sign," my grandfather comments, pointing up to the ceiling with his finger then looking at me and reviewing me.

"I would like to think so. We have a lot of time to catch up on."

My grandfather smiles. "You're able to move on then and try again? Get it right for your next chapter?"

Looking at him, I let out a chuckle. "Still hoping I get married soon, huh?" It comes out light-heartedly.

"Yes. You are my only grandson and a good one. And my clock is ticking. Maybe I could meet her?" he asks, hopeful.

Nodding, I say, "I'll do my best."

I am not letting her go this time. I loved her then, and when I watched her sleep in my arms the other day, it confirms what I always knew. That feeling never went away. Everyone has a "what if" person, and she is mine, except we get a second chance, and it doesn't need to be an *if*.

Gramps takes a sip of water from the glass on the table with shaky hands. "You know, you've never spoken to me about the women in your life." Gramps gives me a glare. "Yes, my boy, I know there must be a trail of them, even if you never told me."

I laugh to myself. I can't say I was a monk, that's for sure, but by no means was I playing the field.

It makes me smile and I scratch the back of my neck. "And your point, Gramps?"

"She is different. I see it in you," the old man reflects.

"She is. She really is." I let it float in the air.

I let his words sink in. After a pause, I look at my watch

and adjust my position in the chair. I need to head back as I have a meeting at four and the drive is a good hour.

"I'm going to head out, Gramps, but I will see you in a few days, okay?" I give him my best look.

"Okay, and maybe, we will actually play a full game of checkers next time," he mentions as he coughs a little. "And Jacob, tell her. I know what you're thinking. But just tell her."

I let his advice hang in my mind.

Arriving at Matchbox, I head over to my friends Leo and Max to say hello. We've all had a few grueling days at work and just want to unwind.

Vaguely, I hear Leo comment to me, "You look like you're finally getting laid. Just keep your puppy-love look out of the negotiation room. I know women tend to make us sappy."

I flash him a sly smile. "Or it makes me negotiate a lot harder. Real hard. Maybe even on the negotiation table."

That comment earns me a respectable laugh from Max. "I like his train of thought. My guess is there's someone here who has you in a good mood." He drinks from his beer bottle but indicates his head towards the bar.

My eyes follow the only line of direction I need, and there she is, next to Max's fiancée, Harper.

And she is gorgeous.

Avery is in a black cotton V-neck dress that clings to her skin at every curve, and my tongue and cock remember them all. I'm positive the dress shows a glimpse of a blue bra, and I already zone in to where I can unzip her. Maybe even with my teeth.

She is laughing with Harper as Nate passes her a drink, and he whispers something into her ear that makes her laugh, and it makes my muscles clench like a man possessed.

Harper, who seems like she may have had a few drinks, drapes an arm around Avery, who plays along with whatever she is saying. Doesn't matter what Harper is doing, my focus is on Avery.

Snapping into action mode, I decide to take the plunge.

"Shall I get a round for us?" I ask the guys, and they nod.

When I reach the bar, Avery has still not turned around. Harper sees me, however, and seems to be up to trouble.

I overhear the conversation and lift a finger over my lips to let Harper know not to reveal my location.

She grins at me as she says, "Come on, Avery, you're single. I'm sure there must be someone who can rock your world."

Maybe it's the alcohol or maybe it's her sarcasm, but Avery cracks out, "Rock my world? You mean like have some guy take me against the wall in the corner?"

Harper sheepishly grins. "Exactly. I even bet there is someone here who could fit that criteria." Her eyes flutter, and she looks at me, entertained. I am certain Avery looks at Harper with inquisition and connects the pieces.

"Jake is behind me, isn't he?" Avery lets out.

Harper gently nods and waves her fingers at me. As she walks away, she whispers into Avery's ear and pats her shoulder, but I hear enough. *Make-up sex, Ave, it's very therapeutic.* Avery slowly turns to me and I am waiting with my best innocent smile.

I order a round for the guys while she takes in the fact that I am in front of her.

"Ooh, looks like they have you on the train to mishaps too," she notes when she hears me place the order for the guys. A lot of whiskeys.

I turn to her. "If we're all on that train, then by all means, why don't you get up on that bar like the other day," I encourage her.

She bites her lip, and it's like she can't help but try and hide the thoughts floating through her head. "I think I have given you a lap dance before." She squints an eye and her mouth oozes pure seduction.

I lick my lips in entertainment. "You did, and I think you have yourself an excellent back-up career."

She shakes her head at my flattery. "Right. My life goals, clearly."

"Want to get some air? Or go straight to a wall for that therapeutic make-up sex?" I ask with an equally entertained and encouraging look.

Avery's cheeks tighten as she blushes lightly, and she lets out a chortle. "Harper's advice is always related to sex, by the way. Let's get some air."

I tell Nate to send a round over to the guys and put it all on my card.

I grab our drinks and lead the way outside to the ledge of the deck and stand admiring the view. An outside heater is on nearby, and fairy lights add to the ambience. We also managed to find a quiet spot away from people.

She grabs her whiskey from my hand and takes a drink and then brings the same glass to my mouth. Taking a sip, I do not let my eyes leave her.

The moment the glass parts from my lips, I speak confidently. "Go to dinner with me."

"What are we doing?" she blurts out. It's a curious, sincere question, and there is a smile she is trying to hide as she sinks her head into her hand.

"Nothing since you won't go to dinner with me," I reply.

She draws in a breath. "I don't know where we left off or where we begin. How do we do this with our history? Be around each other or—I don't know..." She's flustered and adjusts her posture against the railing.

"Come to dinner with me. We can talk or fuck, but we will figure it out," I urge with a cunning look.

She shakes her head. "I do want to see you again, and I don't know what we're doing. Or, I mean, presume that we are..."

Now I have to give her my persuasive grin. "Presume," I instruct boldly, gently touching both of her arms.

She draws her cheeks, trying to keep her satisfaction with my response hidden, but she's failing miserably.

Leaning back on the railing, I look at her and cross my arms in amusement. "No expectations. No time limits. We reconnect."

It's going to be different this time.

"Agreed. And if I need your strong arms to help me off bar tops, then so be it." She shrugs with her lips pursed in entertainment.

"Okay. My arms could be of service. But is that my only body part that can help? I am certain I have some other parts that you thoroughly enjoy." Because I hope she is insinuating what I want.

I want her.

She nearly chokes on some whiskey and looks around to make sure nobody is watching us. "I'm not sure we should go down that route *yet*. Which is a challenge, by the way, especially as I already got a preview of our chapter two, and that was... wow, and, well, just being around you my body doesn't listen." She lets out a deep breath and tries to collect her thoughts. "I'm just not sure heading straight into bed together in that way would be a good idea yet. We still have a lot to talk about."

"It will be different," I assure her.

Because we can go slow or fast. But letting her walk away again is not an option in my book.

Her face changes to trouble. "In what, bed or—?" She dares me now with her head tilted, tapping her glass in her hand. Because I know she couldn't resist that remark.

"You are still something, you know that, right?" I grin.

Her eyes explore me. Her mouth slightly opens as she licks the corner of her lip. She looks away. "Let's see where this goes. We have five years to catch up on. Both of us have had a lot of changes in our lives. While I now know your hands and lips are still as equally talented as before—"

Encircling my arms around her middle, I pull her to me. "I promise I have other talents you need to re-assess."

She gives me a hopeless look and playfully hits my arm. "I'm sure. But maybe we're different people, I don't know."

As much as I want to make it my mission to break her resolve, I respect her too much. It has to be done right if we are in this for the long-term. I think we are.

"Okay. I respect that. You're right, maybe we have both changed. And I also don't know how we do this. But I want to do this. I wanted you then, and already I know I want you now," I let out softly, yet my gaze is hopefully piercing her with intensity.

Her face stays neutral. "You forgot to mention what I want now."

"You want me, I know." I sound a little cocky, yet it makes her struggle not to let a grin form.

"I'm not denying it. In fact, this is a challenge, and I don't know why I'm putting myself through it. Because the other day when I said I wanted you and I needed you to fuck me, I *really* meant it," she admits with defeat. "But slow. We owe it to ourselves after everything," she reaffirms.

Drawing in a breath, I know she has some logic to her point. "Okay. But I think we should try and find our way back to each other, it's all I want."

"Jake I—I can't deny that I enjoy being with you and we definitely still have that chemistry factor, but I just don't know... are we finding our way back to each other? Is it even possible?" she replies with a gentle look on her face, almost somber.

"It's possible."

Taking her hand, I bring it to my lips for a gentle kiss that I hold a few extra seconds as my eyes look down to hers. Her face softens as she slowly nods at my words.

"I believe you owe me a chaste kiss from last night. That is a perfect start to slow," I remind her, and it makes her grin.

"I do." She smiles now.

My hands quickly clutch her face and my mouth dives onto hers. There is no hesitation from her side. Our mouths meet for a slow and soft kiss. We can't help it, and throw the criteria for chaste out the window. Our kiss deepens and my arms wrap around her. I even throw in a little dip, tilting her back as our tongues meet. Bringing her back up, we find a new angle and I can hear her growl in the back of her throat.

Reluctantly pulling away, we look at each other with a knowing look.

"Jake."

"Yes, Avery," I respond like any good future husband of hers would do.

She indicates her head to the door. "Get out of here before your charm persuades me and I decide that you may need to take me against the wall." She straightens her posture and shakes her head with a grimace of enjoyment, which is a good start for our road forward.

CHAPTER FOURTEEN

AVERY

"Really? You perfected a dog cookie recipe? Amazing!" Abby gushes, way too overly excited, as she investigates the white box on the table in front of us in Smokey Java's.

My cousin leans back in her chair, holding her mug. "You know, Jake is donating to the shelter," she says, flashing her eyes.

I roll my head as I know where she is going with this. "Lucas already mentioned that to me the other day when he grabbed a coffee here. And?"

"Lucas says that Jake became very interested in puppies when he learned you donate to the cause." Abby is trying to stir the pot, and she is succeeding, because Jake doesn't do house pets, house plants, or anything that requires water to survive. I am already flirting with the gates of Hell for giving him a goldfish he needs to keep alive.

"Good for the puppies," I fake a smile.

There is a pause.

"Come on, cousin. What's going on?" Abby has a serious tone as she nudges my leg under the table.

Taking a deep breath, I decide I could use an ear.

"Jake, well... he was more than a fling, Abby. Well, we started out as one. We were both working so much that we didn't have time for more. It was fun. Plus, I was only in Chicago for a short time. But it just clicked, *we* clicked. Sex turned to talking, to dinners, and more. Before we could think about where we were heading, I found out I was pregnant. Totally not planned and not great timing." I look to see Abby's eyes widening and her face confused. "We lost the baby, a little boy." It still pinches my heart slightly when I say the words.

"Wow..." Abby inhales a deep breath and gives me a reassuring touch on the arm, taking a few moments to let it sink in. "I'm so sorry. I had no idea." Her voice is full of empathy.

"Miscarriages sometimes happen... We kept it between us. But now that Jake and I finally spoke about it, I feel a little bit of peace, as if I *can* talk about it."

She gives me a comforting half-smile. "I'm happy you have that, Ave. I mean the closure, the peace." Abby leans across the table to give me a hug. "I honestly had no idea."

Abby pulls away and returns to sitting in her seat.

"Nobody had an idea. But here I am still and I'm okay." I tap my nails on the table. "I can't believe he's in my life again and he wants to move on together. I want that too, but I'm scared he'll realize that I don't deserve him. He is so understanding about why I pushed him away. I walked away and let five years go between us."

"But your head must not have been in a good place then. It's understandable."

"Still, you don't run away from each other when it gets tough, but that's what I did," I admit and let my hand go to my mouth to fight back my emotions, which makes Abby rub my arm for comfort.

"You have to trust what he says, and if he says he wants to try again, then believe him. Be kind to yourself. Didn't you mention it was also a casual relationship at that time?"

"Something like that." We never said I love you. We cared for each other deeply, we made plans about the baby, but we never said we loved each other. Maybe it was an unspoken connection, or we both suspected. I wanted to say it because I felt it. Finally, when I felt like we had our future ahead of us, I wanted to tell him, but life had other plans for me, for us. Having an unplanned pregnancy when you've only been with the person a few weeks does something to your train of thought, and for some reason it became my focus.

"Well then. Your second act can be different. Maybe here is your chance for that relationship you could have had if you didn't run away."

My ears perk up because she's right.

"Maybe." I crack a smile, because inside me, a chance is floating around. "I hope so." But that doubt runs strong in my head. At any moment, he could change his mind and decide that I hurt him too much by walking away, or he is too afraid I would only do it again. I don't understand how he couldn't let those thoughts cross his mind.

"Now that I know more about you and Jake, I feel so bad for ruining your night the other night. I really owe you," Abby apologizes, full of guilt.

"Don't worry about it."

After a moment, she kicks my foot and gets a mischievous grin.

"Tell me, what is he *really* like? Because I've heard

stories from Lucas, yet I've only seen Jake ready to assassinate in the courtroom." Abby winks at me.

I let out a laugh. "I shouldn't have given him a goldfish, that's for sure. And underneath that suit is every fantasy imaginable," I admit, getting lost in thought. *Bad thoughts.*

"Ah, so you are thinking about that," she enjoys teasing me.

Leaning into the table, Abby meets me in the middle. Looking around to ensure nobody is listening, I tell her, "His spare key is in my pocket, and I have been thinking of a thousand ways that I can use it. So yes, every fantasy imaginable is going through my head."

She gives me a giddy look.

After talking some more, I head behind the counter and grab another box for Abby. Closing the large white box of peanut butter treats, I hand it to her across the counter.

"Okay, so that is 150 dog treats and 50 human treats." I smile.

"Thanks so much, it'll really be a nice surprise for my visit to the shelter later today." Abby puts her phone on top of the boxes so she can carry all of it to her car.

I should offer her help, but my face is frozen and probably glowing as I see who just came through the door of the bakery. Immediately, his grin tells me he is on a mission and slows his pace towards me.

Abby does a double-take and looks between us. "Right. Obviously, something is brewing here," Abby mumbles so only I can hear. Abby turns her attention to Jake. "Hey, Jake. I was just leaving. I guess I should apologize for stealing this one away the other night. I'm sure you two had big plans." Abby indicates her head towards me, and raises an eyebrow.

Jake looks at her, amused. "Right, dying dog and all."

Abby nods in entertainment. "Exactly. And Romeo is making strides in getting the reunion he wants."

Jake looks at Abby, confused, and I have to laugh. Clearing my throat to clarify, "Romeo is Abby's Labrador, remember?" I remind him, as I know he has been to their house a lot. I wait for him to catch on. "He ate a tennis ball and apparently missed Lucas a lot while he was at his conference," I clarify, and I give Abby a warning look.

"Right. That is exactly what I meant. Bye, guys." Abby grins then heads off.

In truth, her dog's name *is* Romeo, but something tells me Abby wasn't referencing her dog.

I shake my head and grab a cup to put under the coffee machine. "Want a coffee?" I ask with full intention of making a coffee.

"Come to lunch with me?" he invites me smoothly, and my eyes shoot up to his, joy hops up from my core to appear on my face.

I smile. "Found a loophole, huh?"

"You never answered my question about dinner, so thought I would take my chance on lunch." He's coy and tilts his head to the side.

"Okay," I answer. "To be honest, I've been waiting for you to slip that question in like you always used to."

He licks his lips and smirks. "Were you hoping I would?"

My mouth slants to the side. "Yeah... I was."

WE HEAD TO A LITTLE ITALIAN PLACE OFF MAIN Street, nabbing a small circular booth. The candles in the dimly lit room make the ambience the reason travel blogs call this place romantic. Even at lunch, no table goes without a glass of wine to accompany the eggplant parmesan and ravioli.

My eyes search the room after freshening up in the ladies' room, and I see Jake sitting at our corner table looking mighty fine in his gray suit that has a slight sheen. It seems I am not the only one who noticed, as there is a blonde with legs for days, standing over the table talking to him. *Giggling.*

It makes me feel slightly thrown, and I have no right to feel that way. Do I?

Slowly I walk to the table, and when the corner of his eye catches sight of me, his attention turns to me with a smile forming as he stands up quickly. His arm reaches out to wrap around my waist and he gives me a kiss on the cheek. The blonde looks on with interest.

"Hey there, I'm back," I say as I look at the blonde with unease. Letting my fingers play with his tie in a possessive move.

"Ave. I was just catching up with Olivia. We worked together on a case once," he comments, and Olivia seems to be eyeing me as competition. *As she should.*

"Sure. If that's what you want to call it," Olivia quips with her eyes not leaving me. Jake clears his throat as he must pick up on the claws about to come out.

"Nice to meet you." I manage to make it sound convincing... enough.

Olivia gives Jake a flirtatious smile. "You should give me a call again, Jake. Anytime."

"*Actually*, I am quite busy these days with Avery." He kisses me again on the cheek, letting his lips linger to make a statement, and I give Olivia a death stare.

Olivia lets out a hum. "Well, I will leave you to your

lunch then." Hopefully it's her way of saying she got the message, as she pivots and heads away.

Jake scratches his cheek awkwardly for a moment before we go to sit down in the circular booth, sliding next to each other. Truthfully, I don't know how to play this.

Immediately I look at Jake who holds his hands up in surrender.

"It was like three dates," he confesses casually. My stomach turns a little sour.

My eyes are fixed on him as I bite my inner cheek. Finally, after thinking for a few ticks, an exhale escapes me.

"It's okay. I didn't have claim to you for the last five years. It doesn't take a marketing professional to figure out you have the whole image as a bachelor hotshot lawyer with a broody smile going for you." I feel his gaze burning me.

"Is that the image you have of me?" he provokes me with a raised brow. Sliding closer to me, I feel a warm hand has been placed on my thigh under the table. "And I am not a bachelor anymore," he corrects me with a smirk.

My emotions are starting to plan a celebration when I hear those words. There must be a sparkle in my eye as I look at him with a closed-lip smile. But that little balloon of pain somewhere in my chest still reminds me that he deserves more than me. I'm the one who walked away.

Swallowing, I don't know where to take this conversation. He picks up on this. Moving to me, he scans the room, and then his stormy eyes meet mine. He lets our foreheads touch as his hand on my thigh skirts up slightly.

"Let's be clear on something." His tone is firm. "The things you and I did together, every kink, every mind-blowing time we screamed one another's name, I didn't have that again with anyone. Not even close. I don't want to know who the hell has touched you, because it will drive me insane. But I'm going to assume you had the same experience as me: nothing as good as us."

I nod, not letting our heads part, and I am painfully aware I am flooding for him. "Y-You're right," I stammer.

He pulls away, his hand vacating my thigh, and he looks satisfied. Looking around the room, as if the last few minutes haven't happened, he brings up a topic to get our conversation into neutral waters again.

"I'm impressed that you added dog treats to your menu," Jake says. He seems sincere and proud of my work endeavors.

"Yeah, I need to stay creative. There is a pet boutique store that asked me if they could sell my treats in their store, but I don't really know how distribution of product works. Geez, sounds like I'm starting a drug cartel or something," I admit.

He chuckles. "Distributing product? A little. But if you need someone to look over the contract, I know someone." He nudges me.

"Yeah. Me too. He has quite a few skills, actually."

"Oh yeah? Do tell," Jake pretends, with piqued interest.

"Another time. There is an old couple over there who is already staring at us," I warn and indicate my head to the table across the room.

My hands touch the top of Jake's on the table. "I think it's great that you have your own law practice now, your own clients and doing things your way. I mean, look at you. Taking a leisurely lunch on a weekday and the apocalypse hasn't even happened." I take a sip of water. "And you haven't done a disservice to the female population as you are still walking around in those fine suits." I pretend to fan myself.

He laughs. "Thanks. But you have also taken quite a

journey. You traded in your pencil skirts, heels, and blouses —where you had to wear the right bra every time—for casual dresses that send my mind into a million directions of what I could do to you," he warns, and his eyes stray from my eyes to my body.

"Oh? I mean, I still have some of those pencil skirts somewhere in my closet, if that's a deal breaker." I give him a sly look.

"Not at all, but seriously, I am amazed at everything you've done with your business. I *may* have looked up the Smokey Java's Instagram, and it's impressive. Quite a following, and Lucas mentioned that you need to reserve a table for weekend breakfast as the place is packed. Sounds like everything is going well."

I look at him with pride, and also find it funny he looked on my Instagram as he despises social media. I do too, but I only post photos of food. "Thanks," I mumble.

"And you seem to be at a calm and happy place."

Thinking about it, I guess he's right. "Yeah, I am. Now I have a reason to be even more so." My eyes look at him and he knows I mean him, which makes him happy. It makes me happy too, though I'm not sure I deserve it.

During this whole lunch, I can easily flirt with him. But at random moments, that thought that he could change his mind about us lingers in the back of my head. I shake it off.

"By the way, feel free to babysit Freddy the fish anytime. But why didn't you just leave me a plant or jar of cookies?" he asks, amused.

Sliding closer to him, I lean in close. "A cactus was an option, but boring. And if you have cookies at home, then you might not stop by the bakery unannounced. And we decided we like you stopping by the bakery unannounced." I take a sip of wine.

"We?" he asks as he slowly returns his glass to the table.

"Oh, yeah. Tammy the blue-haired waitress thinks you're pretty hot. She let me know her opinion of you. And I want to keep my staff happy, so I need you to keep stopping by," I say, clucking the inside of my cheek. Jake just grins and shakes his head. "Figured she wasn't competition, so what's the harm?" I shrug.

"And what does Tammy's boss think?" He studies me.

"That there is a very good-looking guy that I am lucky to know again," I say, playing with my wine glass stem.

"Anything else?" He moves a piece of my hair behind my ear with his fingers, sending a tingle down my spine.

"A very hot attorney that *maybe* I will kiss today. You know, going slow and all." I drag the sentence out as my eyes move to him. He leans in and kisses my cheek with intent. As if he has a point to prove.

He pulls away slowly to let his lips linger and gently brush across my lips to make me shudder, then creates space between us.

"Someone I've been waiting for," I whisper.

"To do what, Avery?" He speaks in a low voice, with his fingers running through my hair, his mouth moving in. I let my lips dance around his mouth, but not actually touch.

"To take me any way he pleases one day, maybe."

His lips twitch. My mouth drags away to give us some space.

"How have I not gotten you naked in my bed yet?" His eyes lock on me with intensity. Interrogation mode.

Tilting my head to the side, I taunt, "Semantics... technically, I was somewhat naked under your shirt the other night."

"How have I not kissed you today yet?"

"We will get there eventually." I smile softly.

"I really need to kiss you, Ave," he warns, as his hand comes to cup the back of my neck and pulls me towards him.

I respond by giving him an agreeable grin and I claw some material of his shirt to encourage him forward. Our bodies move, our faces connect. He claims my mouth before I have a chance to give it my best shot. Lips and hands touch each other's face, lingering, soft, gentle. That is how it begins. But we deepen it, slanting our mouths in different ways. As if our lips are confirming that we are good to go again, and here is our chance at a second act in our story.

There could be comets flying around us and we wouldn't know, as we are too hooked to this moment.

His hand moves through my hair and we both move in closer as our kissing continues to reconnect us. Our tongues meeting, my arms roping around his neck, bodies snuggling in together.

Finally, we grab air. Clearing our throats and realizing we are in a very public setting.

Grabbing my glass of wine, I hold it out to his. He quickly meets me with his glass.

I straighten my posture in my seat and take a deep breath as I throw on a smile.

"To seeing each other again?" There is skepticism in my voice as I look at him, puzzled if I just made a good toast.

He answers by leaning in and his forehead meets mine. "To getting to do things to you again."

I let out a giggle. "Okay. To seeing each other again, doing things to each other again, and being together again?" I am more confident in my toast, but still add in some fake skepticism just in case.

A sound escapes his throat, and he clinks my glass. "Cheers to that."

We drink our wine then have a quick kiss again, letting our lips brush along each other's jawline as we pull away.

"Now here is the problem with lunch dates. It means there is still the rest of the day to get through, and most likely the other person has plans." I bite my lip and my eyes should be giving him an apology.

"I have many plans for you, so let me pay the check and we go back to my place." His hand reaches for my thigh.

Sighing, I say, "Your hand on my thigh under the table is trouble, I know from experience." My forehead meets his again as I look into his eyes. "I really don't want to take a raincheck, but I can't come home with you for the plans in your head. I have an appointment with a supplier in an hour."

An exhale escapes his clenched teeth. "Slow. Right. I did promise. What about an innocent game of checkers later?"

Our foreheads still have not parted.

"Hmm, sounds harmless, I'm sure." I grin.

An hour later, I listen to the vague details of the supplier. I ignore an e-mail about the award for best small business, and I drop a dozen eggs. My mind is overly occupied with thoughts of Jake. A painful feeling still lingers in me, but equally strong is a desire so uncontrollable that I know what I need to do.

CHAPTER FIFTEEN

JAKE

I LOOK AT AVERY AS SHE SHAKES OFF HER BOOTS AT THE door. We gaze at one another, both with a soft smile as I help her take her scarf off and then unzip her coat. I'm thankful the wet snow touching my fingers keeps me in check, because undressing her multiple layers ups the ante. It's like I am unwrapping a perfect gift.

"I was going to set up checkers but got stuck on a call," I mention. Our eyes seem to be in a trance with one another as I throw her coat to the side bench.

"No, you weren't," she corrects me with a smirk as she knows me too well. Avery gently rises on her toes as her fingertips walk up my chest. "It's cold tonight."

I have to grin slightly. "Promise you, it won't be for much longer." My hands rub warmth into her arms. "How was your meeting?" I ask.

"I don't know. I couldn't focus. I had a lot in my head."

My hand cups her cheek and my thumb rubs her cold milky-smooth skin. "Oh yeah?"

"I've missed you all this time... I'm not sure I mentioned that yet." I hear the vulnerability in her voice. I know her enough to realize she must have been thinking about something significant as her mood is different than at lunch. She is serious, but calm and seems content.

My hands scoop up her own to keep against my chest. "Me too. More than you'll ever know."

Leaning down, I capture her mouth for a warm full kiss, sealing us together.

After a few seconds, she pulls away with her eyes meeting mine full of lust. She leans in to brush her lips along mine, generating a tingle, and she nips me gently with her teeth before looking down at our hands that she interlaces, tugging me behind her, and I follow as she turns to the stairs.

Without words, she guides me by the hand upstairs, and my heart pulses faster as I know I should just let her lead the way. We get to my room where I had left a small light on when I changed earlier into my jeans and shirt.

She turns to me with soft eyes and parted lips. Stepping to me to close the distance, her fingertips brush along my stomach towards the edges of my shirt, her eyes never parting from my own.

Feeling the gentle tickle of her fingers working under the fabric of my shirt, creating an energy of heat between us, I need no further indication. In a quick movement, I reach down and pull my shirt up and off.

Her fingertips gently press against my chest to indicate for me to sit on the bed. But she doesn't need to indicate, I'll take us into the exact same direction she seems to want in this very moment.

She comes to her knees on the floor in front of me. Shimmying closer to me between my legs, she unfastens my jeans, and we slide them off until I am left in my boxer briefs.

Her eyes flick up to meet mine as she rests between my legs on her knees. "You're back in my life, aren't you?" she asks with a voice full of enchantment.

"I am," I confirm, as I lean forward and look down at her.

She tips her head up. "I'm here," Avery whispers in between a gentle kiss on my forehead and cheek. "I'm not going anywhere."

Maybe it's the feeling I've had all day, all week, all five years. Maybe it's the shock that she is in my life again, something I never thought imaginable. But I'm drawn to her more than I thought possible in this moment.

It floats into my mind that we should crawl into bed to fall asleep. Slow, right? That's what she wanted.

...But that is not what I need right now. Nor does she.

Her eyes look into mine and they confirm we both want the same path. My hands grab hers and bring them to my shoulders as I still sit on the bed, so she stands over me.

Looking up at her, my arms encircle around her middle and I pull her to me, letting my head nuzzle into her stomach, and already I can feel her rapid pulse. A soft sigh escapes her mouth when my other hand goes to her bare thigh beneath her dress and moves up her silky skin. My cock grows eager as my hand gets bathed in her warm, damp heat.

Her eyes look at me but do not tell me to stop, and her hand returns to my face where her thumb drags along my jawline. She leans into me, and I can feel the fire between her legs as I stop short of her slit.

I do not want to stop. I need her. I want her.

She picks up on this because she understands me.

When we pull away, we look into each other's eyes for

recognition of what we are doing. Avery places her hands on my chest, and it ignites a fuse in me.

She pushes me to my back, coming to straddle me, as she watches my face to ensure that I am looking at her. Slowly, she pulls her dress up and off to reveal her perfectly shaped globes with nipples hardened, as she skipped the bra today. Her hair falls behind her shoulders.

"You seem to have gotten more beautiful."

And even though she's the one leading us, she is the one who blushes.

Placing my hands on her hips, my body comes to sitting to meet her. My mouth drags between the valley of her breasts and travels up her sizzling hot skin to her mouth, taking note of her rapid pulse.

Leaning in, my mouth captures her bottom lip, tasting her sweetness. Slowly, our mouths meet for a deep and powerful kiss, my hand threading through her hair with her arms looped around my neck.

Our kisses are full of longing, yet soothing, as she circles her hips around my center and presses against my cock. This is all our longing from the years, finally getting a chance to be satisfied. My hands slide up her sides to rest on her ribs, holding her in place so my lips can graze her nipples, softly giving them a lick. A moan escapes her, and that moan sends me on a trail of lust.

A wave of desire shoots through me and intensifies below my navel. Pressure shoots to my groin.

Moving, I guide her, so we are on our sides, staring at each other, getting lost in this moment.

My fingers grab the rim of her panties and tug them down. She finishes pulling them off in a hurry.

Pulling my boxer briefs down quickly, I let my fingers

stroke between her silky folds. Right away, I feel she is flooding for me, and that is the only confirmation I need.

She moves to lie on her back and I re-position over her. "We were going somewhere back then, weren't we?" I ask, because I'm not sure we got all the answers we needed from our talk the other day.

Her hands reach for my face as she opens her legs wide, to welcome me in. "Yeah, we were," Avery confirms, as my tip quickly finds her opening and slides in with ease. "It would have been good where we were going, you were everything to me—ohh," she admits in a near whisper, and her eyes close gently as she sinks into the feeling of me entering her.

I was everything to her.

"I'm not letting you go," I whisper as I move deeper into her, an urge overcoming me to get lost in her body.

She murmurs into my neck as she holds me closer as I settle into her, because she is tight. Without thought, I let my body lead the way, and I fill her up completely with my size, going deep into her until I bottom out and it makes her yelp softly. But before I can study her face to check on her, she meets my mouth with hers.

Her leg comes up to tighten around my waist as her eyes flutter closed for a few seconds. When I feel her ease around me, I pick up the pace, finding a rhythm not particularly gentle, perhaps a little too strong and sharp, but her body arches to meet every thrust, a short sound escaping her as I hit her special spot on each pump. It only makes me pick up our pace, her nails digging into my upper back to brace herself from the force of my movements.

It doesn't cross my mind that this is our first time in years, or that we haven't had a lot of foreplay, or that this is not going to last for more than a few minutes.

This is a natural instinct.

Our bodies leading the way.

Primitive.

Thrusting in and out to make up for all that did not happen.

All those years lost.

Never getting to do this as a goodbye.

Looking into her eyes, they tell me she is on a similar journey. Trying to figure out what this is; closure, mourning, grief, passion, lust, love, our future...

My hand finds hers and entwines our fingers as I place them together on the pillow by her head.

I go harder and faster.

Avery's breathing is ragged, and she buries her head into my shoulder, her inner walls clenching around my cock, squeezing as if she will never let me go. I realize in that moment that she's close; I remember her body, all her wants and reactions are imprinted in my head. The feeling of her warm wet walls milking me sends me to my peak.

Our sounds and grunts fill the air. My hand clasps her cheek, forcing us to stare at one another as she wails with a mixture of pleasure and emotion, her body tilting into my movement.

In that second, I recognize she needed me this way as much as I needed her.

Our mouths fuse together, because we want every part of us to be together in this moment.

I release inside her as her hands fist my hair, and I feel gratification that I can leave my mark in her again. It should always have been only me. My *what if* girl. The one I no doubt never stopped loving.

She holds me and kisses my hair as I stay inside her and

breathe into her slick, sweaty neck with my heart racing, appreciating how beautifully perfect she feels.

We lie there for a few minutes, breathless, saying nothing as she strokes my face, both knowing this is complicated, crazy, needed, love.

Right.

It is only when I feel her body underneath me wiggle a little that I realize I'm still inside her. Slowly, I pull out and roll to my back.

Avery nestles into my arm and lays her head on my chest near my heart that, fuck, I hope she knows is beating for her, wrapping her arm tightly around me. Her fingers make circles on my skin. My arm pulls her closer, placing a kiss on her hair.

Still, we say nothing as we relish our bliss until we fall asleep.

AVERY

Waking as the sun begins to rise and sunlight gently comes through the cracks of the curtains, I feel that our bodies must have shifted during the night as Jake is spooning me, my back to his front, and we fit effortlessly.

Last night was a surreal experience. I've never had sex like that. As if our livelihood depended on it. My mouth did not want to say anything, and all I wanted was him.

Few words, no foreplay, pure comfort, and purely primal.

But it felt right. So right.

Part of me wonders, if I had stayed five years ago, is this what comforting each other would have been like?

Slowly, I barely move my body as a soft mumble escapes

me and my eyes blink open a few times as I look behind me to meet his warm chocolate eyes. His arms tighten around me, his body pressing harder into me.

My hand comes to touch his face and he kisses my palm with a gentle kiss. I slide my hand away and find his arm wrapped around my waist.

We are simmering with each other. Waking up together, slowly and tenderly, is something I've missed.

His hand touches my thigh, and he is reminded that I'm still naked from our encounter a few hours earlier. It does something to him, and I let out a soft gasp when I feel him grow against my back. My hand reaches behind me to feel what I already know.

His body wants me again.

He kisses my neck softly and my eyes meet his.

In that moment, I can't decide if I need him or want him more, but I know he wants me, and I want to take care of him. I want him to have whatever he needs.

The last few days, I realized that the only way to heal sometimes is with the other person. And even though I said slow, all afternoon yesterday, my mind wouldn't stop thinking about us, and the only thing that made sense to me was needing to be with him—like this.

Looking behind me, I let my hand clasp his face and my thumb stroke his mouth.

Every move we make now is like feathers dancing, our bodies making slight adjustments to feel even closer to each other. Our lips brush each other's, sending shudders to my nerve endings.

His lips lead the way to press onto mine.

Our lips meeting is soft, slow, and light. But something overcomes him, and quickly his mouth devours mine and the kiss deepens. Our tongues meet as our mouths slant to get a better angle. The kiss is full of intention and want.

His hand comes to my cheek so he can hold me and kiss me with more force, almost as if he needs me to know how much he wants me. We go for as long as we can, breathing in each other. We are utterly lost in the moment.

I drag our joined hands to my inner thigh, inviting him to move in, guiding his hand with mine to my silky folds, showing him that I woke up ready for him. His fingers touching me to test the waters makes my inner walls ache for him.

It takes no time before his cock is sliding into me because we are both ready. He holds me tight against him as we lie there.

His strong arms make me feel like he won't let go, maybe will never let go. *I hope so.*

It does not matter the circumstances, early mornings are always extra sensitive, gentle, and slow. That is what we do. We take time to look at each other as he thrusts into me, my gentle moans escaping in between our mouths meeting.

I grab his hand and guide it up my body so he can cup and feel my soft breasts as he moves inside me. His fingers find my nipples to pluck, and it sends a wave of sensitivity to my core.

He continues to drive in and out of me, sending vibrations through me.

Our bodies move together in a slow trance, but eventually our pace quickens as he goes deep, and his fingers slide down from my nipples to my clit that he strokes and makes me want to release. We move in sync until we both reach our point of ecstasy.

Holding each other, he stays in me until he has no

choice but to pull out, with the feeling of him left behind and seeping out of me along my thigh.

But just like earlier, I don't care that the bed smells of sex and my thighs are sticky from his cum. I only fall back into his embrace and we both snooze off into a post-bliss state.

At around eight in the morning, I slowly blink my eyes open. Quickly, I realize there is a cold feeling along my side and realize there's an empty space next to me. Managing to move my limbs, I come up to sitting and rub my head.

My eyes shoot up to Jake coming into the room, already dressed in jeans and a dress shirt. His mouth gives me a slight crack in the corner, as if he's recalling last night. He grabs his watch and puts it on as he sits on the bed.

My hand reaches out to touch his arm gently. "Jake," I manage to say, because I don't know what else to say. Last night was unexpected. Not in the sense that it happened, but the fact we made love so intensely that I finally understand how these things can be soul-changing.

He re-angles his body and lets the back of his hand glide along my cheek.

After a moment or two he looks at me with guilt. "We didn't... I didn't use anything."

"It's okay. I'm on birth control... and I trust you," I answer gently, because with our history, that little detail matters a lot. A wave of what can only be described as relief comes over his face, and I wonder why neither one of us even thought about it in the heat of the moment... twice.

"I have to go, but we need to talk." I can't figure out his tone. It's too neutral, too plain. It sends a wave of worry through me.

His look, his gentle nod, in a way tells me something has changed.

CHAPTER SIXTEEN

AVERY

After leaving Jake's, I headed to Smokey Java's. But Jake Sutton does something to me that affects my ability to bake, and all my usual recipes failed at every attempt. I gave up when Jess arrived to grab a coffee.

She's telling me about errands she has to do for Harper and Max's wedding since she has a big role to play. A wedding-shower cake is on her list today, and we head straight into conversation when she asks if I can make one.

"Really, Jess, I'm not a wedding cake specialist. Maybe I could give a recommendation of someone," I insist as I look up from my laptop where we're sitting at a spare table in the café. I'm a baker, not a cake designer.

"But you made ours!"

I choke on my coffee. "Yeah, because that was the 'can you pass the wine and oh by the way we got married here's a cake' kind of wedding cake. Harper is having all the traditional wedding festivities, which requires a beautiful cake that lives up to all her Pinterest dreams."

Jess huffs then pulls up a chair next to me. "How I was

delegated this task, I do not know. Maybe we could do cupcakes? Is that something you would do?"

I can see she's looking at a message from Harper. "If it's really what she wants, then yes, happy to. By the way, Harper seems a little stressed lately," I comment, because I know Jess doesn't mind my honesty.

"She is. Mostly thanks to her mother-in-law-to-be. But hey, can't win them all." She shrugs a shoulder and takes a sip from her coffee-to-go cup. "By the way, I heard you're a finalist for the Sagey for best local business! I bet it's your carrot cake that will seal the deal."

"Oh yeah, free publicity here I come." I try to move us on.

She squints an eye at me. "You have a marketing background. You should have more excitement for this opportunity, surely. Plus, this place has done great. People have to book in advance for weekend breakfast."

"I know, and I guess, well... it is kind of cool." A faint smile appears on my face.

Leaning back in my chair, I cross my legs because my mind also ventures to everything else that is making me happy lately. The thought of the man makes me pulse.

Jess gives me a knowing smile. "Spill it, Avery," she orders with a grin. "I want the Jake update."

"I think we're going in the right direction," I shrug.

"That's a start."

Jess's phone vibrates on the table and she looks at her notification, sighs, and holds up a finger. "Bridezilla wants to know if she can place you and Jake together at the same table at the reception."

"Yeah, sure." Whoa, that comes out too easy-breezy. I should not jump on that ship yet. Not after this morning and the impending *need to talk* conversation that still needs to happen.

Jess bites her lip and types back to Harper. "Good. So, what *is* going on?"

Sinking in my chair, I look at her and debate what to say. "It feels like one step forward, two steps back. I do think we're going in the right direction, but now he wants to talk. It makes me sick just thinking about it, because I felt like something changed in his voice. I mean, maybe I was living in la-la land, thinking that we could talk it out and start again. Maybe he realizes I just hurt him too much. If I were him, I would struggle to forgive me too. But being with him again is like the best piece of cake you could ever have, and you don't want just a piece, you want the whole cake."

Jess straightens her posture and holds out a hand to interrupt before tapping her nails on the tabletop. "First off, everybody wishes they could do things differently, but time machines don't exist, so don't dance around in circles. Just tell him how you feel, and what's bothering you. That guy has a whole new face since he saw you again. At least then he knows, and you can have peace with it. Please learn from my mistakes, I beg of you." She gives me a half-smile with pleading hands. Jess had most certainly danced around in circles with her now husband; it took a while before she admitted her true feelings, even though everyone else knew.

I bite my lip. "You're right. I need to tell him what's bothering me."

———

SITTING AT MY LAPTOP, I WORK ON SOME administration with headphones on, listening to Pete Yorn. Still, it doesn't drown out the sound of a rambunctious child running into the bakery behind me. I take my headphones off and turn my head to see Jake walking behind her and towards me.

My face is surprised yet pleased and slightly confused. Standing up, I slowly walk to meet him in the middle of the bakery. I really want to kiss him, but the child is throwing me off.

"Hi," I greet him quietly.

"Hey," he replies, equally softly.

The child is tugging on his coat. I look at her and then Jake with an amused and bewildered look.

"This is my niece, Stella." He tries to pull her away from his coat with a challenging look. "She is a little hyper after being in the car," he grits through a fake smile that forms on his face.

Ah, of course, his niece. "I can see that. I remember when you used to show me photos when she was a baby." I offer a warm smile.

"Uncle J, Uncle J, Uncle J. Can I have cake now? I want cake," Stella almost sings her way into a tantrum, and I can see Jake is overwhelmed.

Leaning down so I'm at Stella's eye level, I smile at the little girl. "You must be Stella?"

"Yes, are you a special friend that my mommy says Uncle Jake sometimes has?"

I peer up to Jake who has an uncomfortable-looking grin as he scratches the back of his head. I decide to just roll with it and move past that. "Yeah... I'm Avery, and I think I know that you are an amazing artist. Would you like to draw me a picture just like the one that is on your uncle's fridge? And I am sure we can get you a *small* cupcake to have." I empha- size small to assure Jake that the already-hyper girl is not going to get more hyper. I nod to Tammy to come. "Tammy will get you some crayons and you can pick out any cupcake you want."

"Really?" Stella's eyes turn to magic. I give her a nod yes before she skips away with Tammy.

Standing back up, I look at Jake. "Can I get you an espresso... or a double or triple shot of espresso?"

"I may need it. Becca, my sister, has a divorce mediation meeting today. Her sitter cancelled and I was volunteered to babysit."

I nod in understanding.

He gives me a soft smile and grabs my wrist, bringing it to his lips, and he gives me a gentle kiss on my pulse. "I needed to see you and didn't want to wait."

Most certainly a half-smile escapes me. "But you were a little off this morning after we..."

He rubs his chin. "Avery, we need to ta—"

"Talk. Yeah, you established that." I look away from him with a blank look.

Stepping closer to me, he takes my other hand in his. "I'm sorry. I didn't respect your request. I let you lead the way and didn't take into account what you said the other day about going slow." He draws his lips together.

Looking around the bakery, I check to make sure we have no audience. I have to grin. "Exactly, *I* led the way. Wait—is this what has you bothered? What had me freaking out all day?" My eyes blink a few times as I study his face that drops into a realization that he had me worried. "It felt right," I add.

My eyes study his as a wave of relief comes over him, and me.

"It did feel right." Jake quickly grabs me by the waist and pulls me close to him so he can whisper in my ear. "So right." Those words send trembles of relief and joy through my body. And heaven help me, but I want to screw over every health and safety guideline in this place —literally.

"Kind of an almost out-of-body experience, right?" My eyes flutter when I say that as I'm almost bashful.

"Yeah." The corners of his mouth tug to a slant.

We both look at one another with unguarded smiles. Eyes lost, and we are in our own world.

Until Stella comes running to us, jumping and squealing with excitement, forcing Jake and I to step apart.

"Avery, do you dance too? I'm doing ballet classes and I asked Uncle J to dance with me, but he said he doesn't dance."

My gaze moves to Jake who gives me a knowing grin. "Is that so?" I give him a daring look. "You know, your uncle *can* dance, and I think he should show us." I throw a hand to my hip.

Jake scratches his cheek and tries to fight showing his entertainment to this situation. Looking around the bakery, he sees we are pretty much alone as it's mid-afternoon.

"Avery knows I only dance with a stunning woman in my arms."

"Any stunning woman? You had options?" I taunt.

The 6-year-old does not pick up on our adult banter.

"Show me, show me," she bounces.

He grunts in annoyance and holds a hand out to me. In victory, I take his hand.

"Your uncle is really good at leading," I say but look at Jake, letting him know I am insinuating something else. He picks up on it.

We meet in the middle of my bakery and our bodies press together as we sway side to side. Occasionally he twirls me around and brings me back to him.

"Avery is really good at following my lead." He raises a brow at me with his innuendo.

Stella claps then runs off, presumably back to her crayons. Yet, Jake and I stay attached to each other, staring and enjoying the moment.

"You know she lost interest already," I inform him.

"Yeah, but I don't want to let go. Plus, I remember you like dancing. Used to do it all the time around my apartment... even half-naked sometimes," he reminds me as he brings our touching hands to his chest. "Stella is sleeping over. But maybe you can stop by later?"

"Not sure that's a great idea. I mean, your sister has never met me, and now I would hang around her daughter? Plus, it may be weird for your niece that you're dating?" I ask, puzzled.

Jake lets out a sound as he takes out his phone from his pocket and types something into it. "First off, I am her uncle, not her father or mother, so as much as I love the kid, she isn't going to dictate my dating life. Secondly, I would like to think she will be seeing a lot of you in the near future," he lists and holds a finger up as he reads a text on his phone. "And my sister just replied, she doesn't mind."

Laughing, I reposition our embrace. "Okay, you sold it. Shall I bring cookies or cake? What will upgrade me to the cool-person category in Stella's world?"

"Just you, but by all means, show up without any panties on to rock her uncle's world." His arms snake around my waist as he leans back to admire the look on my face.

"I'll take it into consideration."

Jake

My niece was hyper-energized today. The new addition of a goldfish to my home made her day, and then after pizza, she finally headed to bed. She enjoyed having Avery around, and I do too.

Returning to the kitchen after checking my niece is asleep, my arms wrap around a waiting Avery. Kissing her properly without the watching eyes of my little niece, I pick Avery up and sit her on the kitchen counter so we can look into each other's eyes at the same level.

"Ave. I just—I want us to get this right. I want you in my life. Even if it means we need to go slow and reconnect. I'll do it," I tell her as my thumb roams along her cheek.

"I'd like that a lot," she whispers with worshiping eyes of admiration.

She lets out a sigh. "But I don't know how to go slow with you. Our first chapter together was a whirlwind of intensity. Maybe we both need to breathe after having the shock of seeing each other again and all the deep conversations we seem to keep having. Isn't slow the right thing to do?"

"You're right. It was a rollercoaster of intensity last time around. It is logical what you're saying, and again, I will respect that we go slow again if that's what you want. But just know that you are kind of addictive," I admit as my lips graze the base of her throat.

She kisses me again. "And you have a way of demanding what you want and getting it," she reminds me softly as her fingers run through my hair.

"If I recall, you like it that way. And I haven't always gotten what I wanted."

Avery looks at me and her lip twitches because she

understands what I mean. I had wanted her to stay back then, and she did not. She kisses my forehead tenderly.

There is a moment of silence.

"Spend the night? We can just sleep if you want."

She lets out a laugh. "Not sure I should stay tonight. That would take Uncle J's 'special friend' to a whole new meaning." Avery uses air quotes on the special friend part.

"Since we're going slow, we are two innocent souls," I counter as I tuck some hair behind her ear.

"You are convincing. By the way, you are so good with her," she reflects.

"I'm good with her because I can return her when needed." I kiss her forehead.

"There's something I didn't tell you," she admits, her eyes innocent and sweet.

"What didn't you tell me?" I add, my eyes searching her face for an answer. Her head slowly turns to me with her mouth slightly open. I can see her mind is working overtime.

She nods and moves her hands to my face. "I didn't tell you that I was more than crazy about you then, and I don't think I told you that enough."

"I was more than crazy about you too," I repeat as our foreheads meet. Because I feel that is maybe her way of saying she loved me.

The voice in my head is screaming. This is a good moment to tell her. Tell her you love her, and you had mapped a life for us then, and we can map a life together now. Follow your Gramps's advice.

"Avery, I need to be honest. It isn't just crazy, it's lo—"

I'm unable to finish as her mouth captures mine. It seems she got distracted.

Okay, that wild side of her is emerging quickly, because her mouth is devouring mine like I am her last supper.

A match is lit between us and our need overtakes us.

Picking her up, I carry her to the sofa, where she pulls me with her to lying as she wraps her legs around my waist. Her hands grab my t-shirt and she manages to pull it off in record time. The top buttons of her dress come undone with the flick of my fingers, as my mouth attacks her neck.

I can feel she wants this; I feel it because she raises her hips to mine as her dress crinkles at her waist and only a very thin line of sheer silky panties is her guard from any part of my body.

This is now all happening amazingly fast. I may even be getting whiplash from our back and forth the last few days. "Slow, right? Do you want to stop?" I mention it to her, but if she brushes it aside, then I am moving us quickly back on the direct line to my bed express.

She breaks away from kissing my body chaotically. "No, I don't. Not with you. I had a horrible idea to go slow. That's not us. We had five years, that's slow enough. Unless you think we should go slow and wait on the sex part?" she asks, but then doubts it breathlessly.

Absolutely not. Oh wait, I have an unwanted house guest. "My niece," I remind Avery against her lips.

A growl escapes her. "True. Okay. So, this is the universe telling us to go slow? Or maybe we do it quickly on your counter? The pantry? Your garage? Anywhere, as long as it's now." Her smile forms.

I laugh. "Tempting on all counts. But no, we will do it right. I will cook you dinner this week, light a fire, nice music, and no timer, because I have many things I plan to do to you," I explain between peppered kisses on her neck.

"In that sentence, I've learned that you can now apparently cook, you know how to light a fire, and you have become a sappy romantic. All you have to do is mention you're playing lacrosse again like your high school days, and I swear I'll marry you." She's sarcastic which makes my grin inerasable.

"Really? My do-many-things-to-you plan didn't tip you over the edge?" I retort before letting my mouth collide with hers in a commandeering manner.

But she reluctantly puts her hand on my chest, pushing me away slightly to put space between us as she lets out a sigh. But then she quickly jerks up to sitting and brings her loose dress together again to cover herself.

"Oh, couldn't sleep?" Avery asks, surprised. I follow her line of sight and my niece seems to have picked the perfect moment to ask for water. The kid is lucky that she is adorable standing there with a bear hanging from her hand, because she really just ruined our moment.

And I'm already bursting to move me and Avery forward since we can speed past the slow sign.

CHAPTER SEVENTEEN

JAKE

Avery didn't end up spending the night, which was quite disappointing on all fronts, but maybe for the best, since I had to get Stella to school before heading to the office. It was a busy morning, but this afternoon I'm taking a few hours off to go see Gramps. I pull out and swipe my phone and wait for Avery to answer.

I'm already smiling to myself when she answers. "I heard from the guys that you won the local business award, a Sagey. How come you didn't tell me? That's a big accomplishment."

Lucas mentioned it in the guys' text group.

Avery gasps in surprise. "True, I found out literally 30 minutes ago. Geez, Abby and Lucas spread news fast. They were here when I found out. But I'm really not into that stuff. I mean, I get that it's good publicity, so I'll do it. I'm just not looking forward to doing a photoshoot and the interview. Not my scene. Just promise to be waiting for me with wine in hand after."

I let out a short laugh. "You should be proud. But if me

waiting with a bottle of wine will make you happy, then I will gladly do it. And we should celebrate."

"Maybe grab lunch? I can get away from the bakery."

I fumble with my phone as I grab the fob to my car. "I'd love to, but I'm going to see my grandfather. Oh crap, I forgot to pick up some of your brownies—he loves those."

"He's eaten my brownies?" she asks, slightly surprised.

"Yeah. I brought some the other week. The smart man figured out within two seconds that someone special made them."

"Oh yeah?" I can hear the smile in her voice.

"Yeah. You'll have to meet him soon," I mention as I get into my car.

"Well... I actually have a fresh batch of brownies, and if you want company..."

This makes me smile. I love her suggestion. "Are you sure?"

"Yeah. Definitely."

Ten minutes later, I'm picking Avery up from the bakery and she slides into the front seat with a box of brownies. I greet her with a kiss, and not that I care, but her outfit today is perfect for meeting Gramps. She has a simple dark green skirt to her knees, tights, hot as fuck boots, and I'm sure a sweater on under her winter coat. Her hair is down and slightly wavy.

"You're going to drive the senior citizens crazy," I compliment her.

She playfully hits my arm as I drive away.

"How was your morning?" she asks as she settles into her seat.

"I finally got the settlement for my client, so I can't complain too much about today."

Her face lights up and she looks like a child on Christmas Day. "That's great you won the case. Isn't that the case you've been working on for a while?"

Shrugging, I say, "Yeah, but I do win a lot of cases." I realize that came out a little conceited.

"Ooh, someone woke up modest today," she teases. Avery isn't afraid to call me out, never has been.

"He's 94, right, your grandfather?" she asks.

"94 going on 20. He was in good shape for someone his age up until about two months ago and is still chasing the nurses," I reflect with a smile.

"Sounds like real trouble." Avery smiles softly and glances to the side at me. "When did you see him last?"

"The other day, actually."

"Was it a good meeting?"

I contemplate what to tell her. "Yeah. His usual grumpiness, his usual questions."

She touches the outside of my hand. "Did he win at checkers?"

I let out a sigh. "We didn't manage to play; we set the board out, but we didn't finish the game."

"Why was that?" she innocently asks, and I know her eyes have not left me as I focus on the road.

"We talked about you." My eyes quickly meet hers before looking ahead again. She is taken aback.

"W-What do you mean?"

"I told him a bit about us; our history, meeting again."

She takes it all in, but her face is neutral. She looks out the side window.

"Okay." It manages to escape her mouth. "Did it help?"

"Yeah, he gave me some good advice. I'll tell you about it one day."

Maybe today. This all has to be a sign. Reconnect with Avery when my grandfather is weakening, as if she re-entered my life just when I need her.

Our hands interlace on the middle console of the car.

"Thanks for coming. I know he wants to meet you and I'm not sure how much time he has left."

She squeezes my hand. "My pleasure."

THE LOOK ON GRAMPS'S FACE WHEN AVERY WALKS into his room by my side is an unexpected gift. Gramps suddenly looks about ten years younger, and he has a glow about him.

"Is this the magical woman who bakes brownies and puts a smile on your face?" he asks, and I swear the man is giving Avery a thorough once-over that has me slightly concerned.

Avery smiles and holds the box of brownies out.

"Magical she is, and this is Avery," I confirm.

"Hi, and you are the man who gives Jake a run for his money in checkers," she answers. Her face is light and slightly elated. She genuinely wanted to come with me and that means a lot.

I pull up a chair for Avery near my grandfather's bed, and a chair for myself. We take our coats off and get settled.

"How are you feeling? You're looking good today," I comment.

"The same," he responds simply.

"Still refusing medication? Chasing the nurses?"

Drinking from your private stash?" I ask, knowing my stubborn Gramps very well.

"Why do you ask such questions? You're a smart man," he confirms, which makes me grin. "He is a smart man, isn't he, Avery?"

"He is, and not bad-looking either," Avery replies, giving me a glance.

"True. He gets that from me," Gramps quips.

Avery looks at me with a wide smile. "I bet he does. Did he get your charm too?"

"Is he working that on you? He learned only from the best," Gramps replies, and I can see he's happy.

"Are you both done comparing notes on me?" I ask as I pour some water for everyone.

"I don't know, this could be fun." Avery nudges my arm.

"Don't listen to her, Gramps, she can be just as much trouble as you."

"Tell me, Avery, do you enjoy living in Sage Creek now? Jake told me you're not from these parts." He crosses his arms.

"Not from here, no, but I've always had family here. It's beautiful scenery. I'm very lucky to have my bakery in such a perfect little town," Avery answers.

"You want to stay here the rest of your life? Have a family?" he asks.

Avery takes a moment, but then smiles. "Yeah, I do. It feels like the signs are telling me this is where I was supposed to end up," she reflects.

"I think so too." I admire her idea as I interlace our fingers hanging between the chairs, which makes her look at our joined hands with a soft smile.

"Funny how you both ended up in the same place. It'll

be a good story for your grandkids one day." Gramps doesn't hesitate to be bold.

"Maybe so." Avery brushes it off to be polite, I'm sure.

"Is my grandson charming you with flowers? A man should always bring flowers once a week," he instructs.

I let my head sink into my hand that is propped up on the arm of the chair.

"Uh, no, actually," Avery answers.

"Jacob, you need to buy her flowers," my grandfather berates me. "Your grandmother got fresh roses every week on Friday. It kept me out of the doghouse."

Avery's smile grows and she seems to be smitten with my Gramps.

"Duly noted." I'm short and simple.

There is a calming moment in the room. But I feel eyes studying Avery and me.

"It's nice, isn't it? Letting the past be the past and living in the present," he remarks.

His sage advice hits a chord in me, and when my eyes side-glance at Avery, I know she is sinking into the words too.

"Is that what you're doing?" Avery asks my grandfather.

He laughs. "I'm too old, my dear young lady. I have quite a bit of past to remember and not so much in the present. But if I were your age, then I would live in the moment, no time to waste stuck in the past. Soon you will wake up at 94, and a whole life will be behind you that you can dredge through."

I can't decide if that is a morbid thought or peacefully true.

"You're really throwing out some philosophical advice today, Gramps." I let a half-smile form as I adjust my legs.

"Well, it's not every day you bring a beautiful woman to see me. I need to ensure we lock her in, so she comes back."

Avery laughs, and it's a beautiful sound.

Gramps reaches out and touches Avery's arm. She moves her hand closer to him, so it's easier for him to touch.

"I've been trying to get him married for years. He's a real catch, no?" My grandfather speaks to her and clearly ignores that I'm in the room.

"That is our cue to head out and let you get some rest." I guide us away from this conversation that is getting deep again.

"Well, it was nice meeting you," Avery says with a bright smile.

"You too. I hope to see more of you," he replies, then looks at me. "She's a looker and a keeper. Don't let this one get away, young man," he warns me with a stern look while waving a pointed finger at me.

"That's the plan," I remind him.

GETTING BACK IN THE CAR, THERE IS A BRIEF MOMENT as we both breathe and look at one another. I lean over the middle console and let my fingertips brush a few strands of her hair behind her ear. She hums a breath as we stare at one another.

"Thanks for coming."

"My pleasure, really, I enjoyed it. I can see why he has a special place in your heart."

My hand reaches behind her head and my mouth slants and plants on her bottom lip to kiss, before moving into a deeper kiss, and she makes that sweet sound, deep in the back of her throat that I love so much.

Pulling away, my thumb brushes her lip. I sigh that I have to break away from her, but I need to get this car moving.

As we drive away and head onto the road back to Sage Creek, I ponder over the conversation with Gramps and Avery.

"So, you and Gramps mapped out your life, it seems." I smile to myself.

Avery rolls her head against the headrest in my direction. "Seems so."

"Was any of it true, or were you humoring him?"

An audible exhale escapes her. "I think it's true. I mean, at least the part about kids and marriage, plus being happy where I ended up." She shifts in her seat to turn in an angle towards me. "I guess... we never actually talked about that stuff last time around. We didn't talk about wanting kids, we were just unexpectedly pregnant. And we didn't talk about marriage. We were having a fun summer, and then our focus was on the pregnancy."

An ache in my heart feels like now is the time to tell her that it was very much on my mind.

Instead, I suggest, "How about tonight, we have a night in. Order in some food, talk, and see where the night takes us..." I glance over at her with my best charming look.

She chortles and smiles. "You really are a romantic. And I would love to, but I'm meeting the girls to talk wedding preparation for Harper."

"Why do I have a feeling wine is involved in that meeting?"

She shrugs. "There *could* be a glass or two. But what about a rain check for tomorrow night?"

I turn on the road. "I will most likely be home late. Have to head up north with Leo for a meeting."

She gently strokes my hand on the middle console. "It's okay. We have time."

I nod and we both focus on the scenery of snow-covered pine trees passing by.

Her breath catches before she speaks. "It's what you want eventually, right? Kids and all of that?" I feel like she is double-checking that we are both on the same wavelength of where version 2.0 of us could lead.

"Yeah, I think so." I know so. And I want it to be with her.

I continue to drive for what feels like minutes in silence.

"Live in the present," she mumbles my grandfather's words as she looks out the window to the side. I have a strong feeling her mind is heavy with everything she's trying to figure out. I'm not sure what, but for some reason I understand her.

CHAPTER EIGHTEEN

JAKE

THE MEETING UP NORTH WITH LEO TOOK LONGER THAN scheduled, which means I'm arriving home later than planned and I am tired. Avery's car was outside, but she should be sleeping already. Taking off my tie as I go up the stairs and sighing from exhaustion, I'm excited to get a good night of sleep and crawl into bed to wrap my arms around a sleeping Avery.

But as soon as I enter my bedroom, I am wide awake and ready for a marathon.

Avery lies provocatively on my bed in a short silky black robe that is partially open, enough to see her upper thigh on display.

Throwing my suit jacket to the chaise lounge on the side, I begin to unbutton my shirt. "I need you to always be waiting for me when I come home," I demand.

Coming off the bed, she walks to meet me in the middle of the room.

"Like this? Or like this?" She gives me a seductive look as she lets her robe fall to a pool at her feet. She is standing there in only her fancy lingerie, and she looks beautiful. Angelic yet naughty, and I want to go deep into her.

"Your baby pink bra and panties are going to get me into serious trouble. I might need my own attorney to get me out of the criminal things I plan to do to you," I tell her as my eyes lock on the sight in front of me.

"No touching tonight," she jokes with an entertained look.

"I'm going to pull an objection. You see, you said no touching, but you did not clarify me directly. It wouldn't hold up in court," I tell her, with my eyes giving her a knowing look.

Avery stands up on her toes and kisses me quickly on the lips, but it's enough to tip me over the edge. And I'm unhinged.

The past few days we have been around one another, but we didn't have opportunities for this. No, instead we were growing closer in other ways. But now, the moment is ours.

My body pounces on her, and my lips crash down on her own. My arms wrap around her waist and press her body against mine. I kiss her hungrily and possessively as she is mine again. Her hands hurry to my face to hold me so she can kiss me deep, as she re-angles her lips. I let her tongue travel in my mouth, stroking against mine.

Reluctantly pulling away, she takes my hands, guiding me back to the bed like she owns the place, and she can. She can have whatever she wants, I will give it to her. Five goldfish, my Audi Q, even though she is a horrible driver, my house, kids—a lot of kids—hell, I will even get a puppy with a bow.

She flops onto the bed with a squeal of delight. Leaning back on her propped arms, she watches me as I take my pants off in a swift movement. "Move faster," she demands playfully.

I get on the bed on all fours with a smirk to warn her, then instantly, I grab her ankles and pull her to the middle of the bed. My head dips down and places kisses on her inner thigh as I work my way up, her hips tilting up in response.

"Jake," she lets out a soft moan.

"I need to taste your beautiful pussy," I growl against her skin.

She bites her bottom lip in satisfaction as I hook under the edges of the lace and peel down her panties, her legs lifting to the sky. Throwing the scrap of cloth to the side, my hands touch her smooth skin as she opens wide for me.

My mouth has perfect access to her wet center. I quickly flick my tongue on her swollen clit and then delve into her, her taste making me slightly delirious because she is sweet and aroused, and only for me.

I can't wait for all of that to coat my cock as I fill her up. My finger goes along her folds and finds her clit that I quickly flick before bringing a finger inside her. In no time, my finger and thumb are working her.

The room fills with the sounds of her pleasure, which only encourages me. My hands spread her thighs farther apart so I can reach her better. I know what she likes. Between my fingers and tongue, I have her body curving to me; hips rising and her moaning my name over and over with her hands clawing the sheets.

"You have to stop," she gasps. "I want to come with you, and I am going to come soon," she clarifies.

"So, you'll come twice, I remember you can do it," I remind her of the facts as my fingers still move inside her.

She lets out a short laugh and then squirms under me, trying to move away from me.

"No," she says firmly with a seductive grin, as she comes to her knees to meet me in the center of the bed. Her hand reaches for my boxers, diving in to feel my hard length. "I want us to come together or I am not going to come at all." It is not a request; it is a demand.

"Do you have any idea what your words are doing to me?" I ask, with my eyes roaming her up and down. She lets out a grin. Then our lips crash onto each other's and I know she tastes herself on my mouth. Pressure in my cock electrifies in intensity from that thought.

My mouth finds her neck, and her head falls back, which makes her offer her breast to me and my head moves down to her smooth mounds. Moving the fabric to the side, I tease her nipple and I get an instant reaction from her as she arches into my body with a moan, her body pressing into my cock.

She quickly rises up on her knees and unhooks her bra from behind, so it falls to the bed, making sure I watch, and then slowly she lies down. I hover over her and cage her in under me. Her face is a masterpiece with her look of desire.

Her hand curls around my cock firmly and strokes my length. "Inside me now," she orders, her eyes focusing in on mine.

The strength of her grip on my cock when she touches me makes me want to come so hard. After stroking me a few times, she rolls to her side to switch positions.

Encouraging her to come close, we shift to sitting and she straddles me. In one movement, her wetness drowns me as she works the top of my cock, moving up and down on me.

"A perfect fit," she gasps as she moves in slow pumps.

With every flick of my tongue on her nipple, she clenches tighter around me.

"Fucking perfect, but I need to take you," I warn.

I roll us back and she is under me. Hooking under her knees, I bring her legs over my shoulders to enable me to reach inside her even deeper. A sound escapes her on every pump as I am hitting her sensitive spot.

"Jake, oh God." She tries to breathe through her moan.

I want to look into her eyes and be in control, but her eyes are hooded closed as she gets lost in her pleasure.

"Open your eyes," I request as I slow the rhythm so I can take in this moment between us.

Her eyes blink open and her hands come to my back to press me deeper into her.

"Tell me you want to come." I go as deep as I can.

"I want to come," she admits between a euphoria of breathing. "But I want you to come more."

Fuck, she is about to send me over the edge and our pace quickens again. I interlace our hands as her O's pick up frequency and fill the house, I know I am about to make her scream.

She does.

Not only screaming but quaking around me and shuddering as she reaches her high. Her coming is enough to send me over the edge too, and I let go.

Our eyes meet and then our lips crash against each other, moaning into each other's mouth. I unload into her and it makes her release a sweet sound. My climax grips me and twists me as it so powerful. I can feel the jerkiness of filling her up, first in a swoosh, then drop by drop.

We stay entangled. Recovering our breathing and kissing each other's neck, shoulders, face... any inch of skin our lips want, our eyes meeting for connection.

Her hands come to hold my face and an innocent smile erupts. "You feel so good," she whispers, and I kiss her lips.

"I'm going to be coming in you all night. You're mine," I warn her, because it is some human evolution that makes me want to mark her as mine over and over. It makes her erupt in a smile too.

A moment later, her face softens. "I'm not dreaming, am I? This? Us?"

My fingers brush a few strands of her hair behind her ear as I look into her eyes where she lies under me and I am still inside her. "Not a dream. We are together again," I whisper before kissing her with confirmation.

I begin to pull out, but she stops me. Her hands grip my hips, her legs wrapping tighter around my waist again.

Her hand moves to hold my face. "I love you." Her voice is light, almost as if she knows she is laying her vulnerability on the line.

Her words are everything to me. I have been waiting a long time to hear them and say them in return.

Worth it.

A smile forms on my face. "I loved you then and I love you now."

Her face beams as we meet for a kiss. After repeating the words several times, we find our way into another wave of pleasure, knowing full well that we are past the point of no return, yet something in me wonders if I need to be even more honest with her.

CHAPTER NINETEEN

JAKE

WE COLLAPSE ON MY BED, BOTH CATCHING OUR breath, staring at the ceiling, naked.

"I don't even know what position that was," Avery confesses, flabbergasted.

"Me neither, but it is staying in our repertoire," I decide, and my arm reaches for Avery and I pull her against my chest, tucking her head under my chin. We've been adding a lot of things to our repertoire the last week. Luckily this morning, we can recover fully as Avery doesn't need to get up early to be at the bakery—her early-morning schedule is a killer.

Last night was kind of crazy. We decided to open a good bottle of wine, watch the video we once made of our younger selves, and that obviously did something to us, as this morning we rounded off our fifth round of mind-boggling sex.

"I'm not sure what I need more, a shower or breakfast," she ponders.

My fingers graze the skin on her back. "Definitely

breakfast. A shower would be useless, as I have some post-breakfast plans for you," I warn her.

She snorts. "Sounds dirty, *and how* do you have so much energy? Have you not aged at all?"

"Avery, I swear I will spank you again. I am not that old," I remind her as I squeeze her close to me before she hops out of bed and throws on some underwear and one of my work shirts.

I tell her, "I'll be downstairs in a few minutes. Need to quickly check my work e-mails—I know, I know it's the weekend." I wave a hand in the air.

She smiles at me from the doorway. "It's okay. It's actually the first time I have heard you mention work on the weekend since I met you again. Times have changed." It comes out soft.

She's right. As she walks away, I think about how life has changed. We're both at a calmer place in our lives, a better, more balanced place.

Grabbing my phone from the charger on my dresser, I do a quick scroll. Nothing crazy, nothing that needs immediate attention.

A loud shriek fills my house. A shriek or scream from Avery is not a memory I enjoy, but it wasn't that kind of sound, and for some reason I feel like she'll tell me she saw a spider and needs my strong arms to save her. Quickly I run downstairs.

As soon as I'm at the bottom of the stairs and arrive in the kitchen, I see the two women of my life.

"Well, well, well," our guest says, leaning against the counter with arms crossed, a very satisfied grin on her face as she assesses her nails. "Look at this scene. Imagine my surprise when a half-dressed woman came down the stairs to make you breakfast."

Going to Avery, she moves behind me as she is still only in my shirt.

"Imagine my surprise when my sister uses a key she was supposed to return months ago," I utter in annoyance.

"Avery, this is my sister Becca. Becca, this is Avery," I do the introductions, but I am not impressed. Even though I'm not keeping Avery a secret—hell, I will hire a blimp to display the message across the skies that we're together—but meeting family can be a big deal.

"Hi again. Becca introduced herself after I came down the stairs and was *very* surprised to find someone in the kitchen," Avery clarifies.

"Judging by the fact you are also half-naked, then I would say you both had a really good night," Becca chuckles to herself.

"We did, actually, so unless you would like the play-by-play, then—"

Avery cuts in, "And that's my cue to excuse myself and change into clothes that my parents would consider respectable. So, I will be right back and then we can, uhm... breakfast, maybe?" Avery says, unsteady in her voice as she walks backwards towards the stairs with her long fingers dancing. Then she quickly turns around and heads upstairs.

As soon as Avery is upstairs, I look to Becca who is pouring coffee from the coffee pot.

"Maybe go easy on the coffee? I don't need you extra hyper around Avery," I plead as Becca sips from her mug and goes to sit at the counter.

After grabbing a clean shirt from the laundry room and returning to the kitchen, I catch up with Becca about Stella, her divorce, and demand I have my key back. She obliges, eventually.

When I hear Avery come down the stairs, I give a stern warning to my sister. "Becca, be nice."

"Relax, little brother, I won't embarrass you. I'm just going to—"

Avery smiles. "Hey. So, let's try this again. I've heard so many things about you. It's nice to finally meet you."

She comes to my side and I drape an arm around her, pulling her in front of me. She is in a red-and-white flowered cotton dress that goes to her knees. It would look great bunched at her waist while I have my way with her, but her leggings are in the way.

"I am indeed the sister of this guy. And you must be the *special friend* who was getting half-naked with my brother for my daughter to witness." Becca's grin is giving me a warning, and I shake my head.

Avery's eyes look at me a bit shocked, but then I see she finds it entertaining.

"Guilty?" Avery confirms and asks at the same time.

Becca laughs. "Relax. I find it cool, actually. You are the first woman that my brother had the guts to keep over when his niece is present, which is an accomplishment, as I am pretty sure the list of women in his address book is ridiculously long."

"Whoa. Simmer it down," I warn my sister before I take a sip of coffee.

"What? I can be honest. I mean, just like I can say that a woman who knows how to bake also knows how to use her hands." Becca clears her throat and raises an eyebrow. Avery can't help but let a laugh escape.

"Is being abrupt a family thing? I see some similarities between you two," Avery comments and motions between us.

My arm goes around her. "I don't know. We're still

convinced Becca is from another planet. We just can't figure out which one."

"Stella is a really sweet kid. I like her free spirit," Avery compliments with a smile.

Becca smiles with pride. "Yeah, she is. She's outside playing in the snow. She has not stopped talking about the goldfish and that Avery knows how to bake cookies. You're like a magical wizard to her. I mean, really, what the hell is happening? My brother has a goldfish?"

I let out a laugh. "I'm trying to be a softer soul."

"It was a test, really. If he could keep the fish alive for one week then I would agree to dinner with him." Avery is sarcastic and gives my sister an agreeing grin, which my sister loves.

"So, Jake mentioned that you two knew each other already. What's the story?"

"I lived in Chicago while I worked on a project. It was only a few months, though," Avery explains.

"Oh, so I guess that was a few years ago, since Jake boy here moved to Colorado a while back." Becca adds another packet of sugar to her coffee.

"Five years, actually," I let out.

"It was a summer," Avery smiles.

Becca leans back in her chair and studies me. Letting her eyes float between Avery and me as she connects some dots.

"I'll be damned," she mutters.

Avery looks at me a little lost. My eyes blink, hoping Becca doesn't do something stupid.

Avery's phone goes off and she looks at the screen. "Sorry, I need to take this—it's the bakery." She seems unsure but turns to me and I nod. "Be right back."

The moment Avery is out of sight, I lean into the

counter. Stella comes in from outside and goes to the living area and turns on the television to some kids' show about magic ponies.

"Becca," I hiss.

Becca leans across the kitchen island. "It's *her*. The one you were going to propose to, but never did."

"Will you keep it down?" I warn.

"She broke your heart and walked away. Now, you want to try again." Becca is charged.

I bite my lip. "First off, she doesn't know I was going to propose, and trust me when I say there was a good reason for why she walked away," I explain.

Becca studies me.

"Becca really, can you let it go?" I urge.

Becca presses, "Can't I watch out for my brother?"

"Yeah, you can, but trust me when I say I'm fine," I assure her. I scan the room to make sure Avery doesn't witness this interaction.

"How do you even remember I was going to propose to someone?" I ask, leaning back against the counter.

"Remember that one Thanksgiving when I said you need to stop serial dating? You said that you weren't always like that and that you were even going to propose to someone before. I pressed and you told me it was some girl you met in Chicago and it was a few months together," Becca tells me, and it all comes back. I did give her vague details when she tried setting me up with some chick from her spin class.

"Yes, okay, it's Avery," I admit.

"Why is it so different this time?" she asks.

"Because she isn't pregnant," I blurt out to my hounding sister.

Becca is speechless.

"W-what?"

Letting my fingers rest on my forehead as one hand finds my hip, I tell her. "She was pregnant last time, one of the reasons I was going to propose. We lost the baby and that's why we ended." I stare endlessly into my coffee mug.

Becca closes her mouth. She gets up out of her chair and walks to me, leaning against the sink beside me.

"Why didn't you tell me? I would have been there for you."

"We didn't tell anyone, and please don't bring it up to Ave. So yeah, that is also the reason she doesn't know I was going to propose. Life had different plans for us," I reflect somberly.

Becca touches my hand. "Maybe you should be open with her, it sounds like it bothers you that she doesn't know."

"Geez, you and Gramps hand out the same advice." I can't help but feel sentimental and also have an itchy feeling that my sister is right.

Becca smiles softly. "Really? You spoke about it with him?"

I nod.

She slants a shoulder. "Then follow his advice. He was always the smart one," she encourages.

"I will."

Avery returns to the kitchen. "I'm back." She smiles at me to let me know she is okay with all of this.

Walking to her, my arm wraps around her shoulder. "You will be seeing a lot of Avery in the future," I announce to Becca.

"This is crazy! I mean, a month ago you were single and living a bachelor's life. What is happening?" Becca asks theatrically yet throws on a smile now.

"It was just meant to be this way."

Becca looks at me. "Fine. Not like you should take advice from me since I'm in the middle of a divorce. But I just want you to be happy. If it's with Avery, then... okay." Becca seems to be calming down and is genuine.

I look at Becca and indicate my head to Avery.

Becca continues after rolling her eyes. "Welcome to the family, Avery." Becca throws on a smile.

Avery tries not to laugh. "Thanks. I love your authenticity."

In that moment, I am grateful that Avery has the ability to not let people affect her so much. Well, everyone except me. I would like to think that I affect her a lot.

"Okay. Shall I get us all some breakfast?" Avery claps her hands together.

Breakfast with these two women? Something tells me this will be a long morning.

Avery got breakfast together in no time. Eggs, bacon, and she even threw together some corn muffins at record speed like the pro she is. After eating breakfast and talking about topics that were initiated by my niece—so, Freddy the fish, ballet, and ponies—Becca goes to grab their coats as Stella runs around.

I let an exasperated exhale leave me as I close the fridge to put away the butter. Avery gives me a reassuring smile as she wraps her arms around me.

"You survived my sister," I compliment her, kissing her hair.

"She isn't that bad. I could get used to her. I guess I should probably tell my brother too, at some point, about this change of events." She motions between us. "It's not a big deal, but maybe an adult thing to do."

I nod, and even though it's been years since I spoke to

Greg, I offer, "Probably, yes. Want me to call him and speak to him?"

"How very chivalrous of you, but it's not needed." She grabs her phone, typing a message. "Plus, it's already done." She wiggles her phone in the air.

My phone pings, and I pull it from my pocket. I look at it and then Avery. "You didn't." I shake my head in entertainment. Then type something so Avery's phone pings.

New Group Chat:

Avery: Hey, Greg, guess you have a shift. Just wanted to let you know that I have a boyfriend. You know him, actually. Remember Jake from your college days? Yeah, so, we are together, and actually five years ago we were together too. He rocks my world etc.

Me: Your sister is really something, you know that?!

Greg: Okay. Did I have too long of a shift, or did I read this correctly? A little crazy, but sounds legit and congrats!

Avery brings her hand to my face and kisses me gently on the lips.

"I hope you have more plans than an innocent kiss on the lips," I prompt her.

"What, like tying me to your fridge so you can have your way with me?"

"I will be bringing you to your knees," I tell her as I dive in for a deep kiss.

My sister clears her throat when she enters the kitchen in her coat.

"Sorry to, erm... interrupt? Thanks for letting us crash your breakfast. I know Avery doesn't get too many Saturdays off, but Stella is super happy now. We're going to be on our way," Becca tells us genuinely.

Just then, Stella comes running into the kitchen and pulls on Avery's skirt.

"Avery, what's this?" Stella holds out the small box that has been jeering me from in a box on my shelf for five years.

My face drops, eyes widen, and that is nothing compared to Avery's face turning pale with eyes bugging out.

Becca, who manages to grab Stella in record time and realizes what is about to transpire, quickly jumps in. "Ohh-kay then, that is our cue to leave. Stella, we are going to go and leave Uncle Jake and Avery alone. I think they need to, uh, talk…"

Becca gives me a gentle smile as she takes the box out of Stella's hands and places it on the counter. She mouths sorry as she drags Stella back towards the front door. When they're gone, I turn to Avery who is speechless and motionless.

After a solid few minutes of earth-shattering silence, I bite the bullet. "This isn't how I thought this conversation would go."

"What conversation?" she asks, blankly looking forward, leaning against the counter, and her face gives no indication of what emotion she must be feeling.

"The 'I'm also to blame about the way we ended' conversation. I made mistakes; I have regrets."

"You did everything right. You wanted to be there for me, you didn't want me to go; you respected my wish to leave. And now you are letting me have a second chance."

"…And I could have asked you to marry me no matter what. I still could have told you I loved you, like I had planned to," I confess. "But I didn't."

Her eyes shoot up to me. An exhale escapes me as I didn't plan on saying that like this.

"What do you mean?"

Christ, her poker face is killing me right now.

A deep sigh escapes me. "I am trying to be honest with you." I pause and debate how to continue. "I was going to... uh... I was going to ask when we planned to go away that weekend."

She must be recalling the timeline and her eyes well. Her hand grabs her hair, trying to let the information sink in. "But you never got to." It barely comes out.

Nodding softly, I reach out to her, but she steps back.

"I need some air."

CHAPTER TWENTY

JAKE

"What woman wants to hear that someone was going to propose to her, but didn't?" Lucas shoots out before he drinks from his bottle of beer. He's sitting on a reclining chair in my living room and props his feet on the coffee table.

Avery went for a walk, but then texted she needed to stop by the bakery and wanted some space. I called an S.O.S. to Lucas because I could use an ear.

A deep sigh escapes me as I sink into the sofa in my living room. "It's called honesty. Trust me, I know the timing did not work out for us. But in the span of one week, we went from planning our future to her walking away. I thought I had more time," I defend as I begin to pace the living room.

"I'm not sure telling her how you felt then is the best move. If it was true feelings, then maybe she doesn't want to be reminded of what she walked away from?" Lucas offers with an unsteady voice.

My hands glide through my hair as I let out a growl.

"I fucked up," I admit.

"You didn't fuck up; you just maybe need to work on your wording, which is kind of surprising since you use a lot of words in your job. Like, a lot," Lucas reminds me.

I give him a scowl. "Ave isn't my job. She is everything else in my life."

Lucas studies me for a second. "You can turn this around, man. I know you can. Just maybe focus on the present."

I bite my lip and think about it. "You're right, the now," I agree.

"Great. So, you stop focusing on the past maybe?" Lucas prompts.

"She brought it up," I defend, which is a low move even for me.

Lucas holds up and wiggles the black ring box. "And you still hold on to an engagement ring from five years ago." Lucas gives me a knowing look.

"I didn't know what to do with it. I kind of threw it into the box of everything else I lost at the end of that summer." I scratch my head.

"Fair enough, but that's then. What are you going to do now?"

I grab my beer from the coffee table and consider my options. "You're right, give me the box," I request and hold my hands out. Lucas throws it to me, and I catch it.

"You're going to propose?" Lucas looks at me, confused.

"Nah... not today." I tilt my head to the side.

SITTING WITH MY GRANDFATHER, I HAVE A COFFEE IN my hand. We are sitting on chairs next to the window.

"What's troubling you?" he asks as he studies me.

I blow out a deep long sigh. "I unintentionally hurt Avery, I think."

"Oh?" Even for an old man, his tone goes high.

I look to him. "I was going to propose to her five years ago, but it didn't work out. She never knew until Stella accidently found the ring box yesterday morning."

He chuckles. "My great-granddaughter can be a show-stopper." He coughs a little. "Hmm. She is more than an ex-girlfriend, isn't she?"

I nod yes.

"She looks at you the way someone who you will spend your life with is supposed to look at you," he mentions, and his words float in the air as I think about it.

"I feel like the past keeps coming back to us." I look far ahead out the window at the winter day.

Gramps laughs to himself. "So, you're both not following my wise advice of living in the present then."

I turn my attention to him, because he is right.

He continues, "You two don't need to make it so hard for yourselves. If you both want to be together and try, then don't overthink it. Create new memories."

Reflecting on that, I must agree. "We have maybe been overthinking it. We just want it to work and don't know the right way to find our way back to one another."

My grandfather reaches for my arm. "You already found your way back to one another. That's clear."

My lips tug at that, as it's true. "I should just lay it all out for her. No more keeping it inside."

"You could buy her some flowers too and maybe throw in a ring." He smiles.

"One day. Okay, Gramps, I'm off. I need to go to Avery. Knowing her, she is burying herself in baking." I stand up and throw on my coat that was hanging on the back of the chair.

"Perfect wife material then."

I shake my head at my grandfather's humor. "Soon," I remind him.

AVERY

My bowl of cookie dough looks a little lifeless, probably because I gave up halfway through. A reflection of my mood.

"Here, have a tea," Abby offers as she hands me a mug and comes into the kitchen at Smokey Java's. "You've been stress baking," she comments.

I nod gently before another tear falls. Abby brings her arms around me for a hug.

"I know. It happens when you get a reminder of what you walked away from," I explain as I sip from the mug.

"You mentioned Jess's advice about laying your cards on the table. Did you lay all your cards on the table?"

I let my head flop side to side. "I didn't think I needed to as it was going the direction I wanted it to." I get top marks for admitting I love him, but I didn't tell him I only see a future with him, or that I'm scared that one day he will wake up and realize he's too scared I'll hurt him again.

"Well, that wasn't the right play," Abby informs me.

"Ya think?" I tell her sarcastically.

"Just tell him. And trust me, the guy is crazy about you."

"I know that too. Maybe it's more that I keep feeling this guilt because I left. The last few weeks, I've realized that maybe everything happened the way it was supposed to, and we did find our way back to each other. But being reminded of what could have been still stings a little. I don't want to feel guilty anymore. We've spoken about it. He doesn't need to walk on eggshells around me, which is why I think he never told me about the ring." I try to understand as I play with the wooden spoon in the bowl.

"You should let the guilt go. You're both heading on a really good path forward. The future sounds good," Abby tells me attentively as she touches my arm for reassurance.

"I know. Just sometimes to get to the future you need the right closure from the past."

"Do you have it now?"

"I don't know." All my questions have been answered, we have talked about everything. I know the changes in our life are good, and I know we're still meant to be together. But I can't shake the fact that I hurt him. It still taunts me silently in the corner of my heart. That ring was a reminder.

"Listen, I need to go. Are you sure you're okay?" Abby asks as she grabs her coat.

"Abby," I give her a pointed look. "It's the middle of the afternoon, you moped around with me for a good hour, and I have a bowl of cookie dough in front of me. If that doesn't scream that I'll be okay then I don't know what will." I offer her a weakened smile.

20 minutes later, and I've managed to salvage my cookies. Looking around the kitchen of Smokey Java's, a deep sigh escapes me. Then I quickly shudder when I hear someone behind me. Yet, I'm not scared because I know who it is. My eyes close then open, as I feel him walking towards me, and already I feel like I am evaporating out of my skin.

"Not sure I should be back here knowing our history of counters, wooden spoons, health and safety, and the fact that I may be the last person you want to see. But I'll take my chances," Jake announces lightly as he places a bouquet of roses on the counter in my sight. The gesture makes my lips tug.

"I know a good attorney to get me out of the health and safety fine. Plus, he seems to be listening to his grandfather's advice on flowers."

A soft sound escapes his mouth as his hand touches my arm gently, forcing me to turn to meet his eyes.

"Yes, because I'm not leaving until you hear me out."

My eyes flutter up. His eyes hold mine as his fingertips gently touch my arm.

He is so incredibly handsome. Different to when he's in a suit. Casual Jake is equally sexy. Jeans, dark blue t-shirt that stretches enough to see his hard chest, his watch. Those sparkly brown eyes holding my gaze. *This man.* The guy who always showers me with a protective and leading nature, who gets my humor, brings out my sensual side, and who I want to love forever. I just want to throw my arms around him and tell him.

But he doesn't give me a chance.

"I think we have an incredible future together, and we have gotten so much closure the last few weeks on so many things. We both have regrets for how we ended. But maybe we should cut ourselves some slack, because our beautiful surprise was just not meant to be. And it hurts because there was nothing we could have done to change that. It was your choice to walk away. But I also made mistakes. There are so many things I didn't tell you. I should not have given up so easily and should have followed you, begged, I don't know, done anything to bring you back. But I didn't. I didn't even tell you I loved you when I was madly in love with you. I never stopped."

He grabs my hand, but my eyes don't leave him, and I

am speechless. My eyes burn a little from the tears welling up, and my heart aches from the new flicker of happiness starting.

"Now, I just want you to not walk away again, and I know that if you try, I won't let you. We didn't have the last five years, but here we are now. I'm not going away, and all indications are that you're not going away either. I made my choice the moment I saw you again, I want to move on with you. I want it all again with you, I want new things with you. I want to be the everything that you dreamed about. No more could-have-hads, we have it now." His heartfelt monologue is honest and answers all my questions.

Perfection.

No wonder he must be good at closing arguments in court.

I step closer, but instead he stops me again with words.

"I'll give you space, but please think about what I just said... we have it all now." His thumb quickly grazes along my cheek before he turns and leaves, giving me no time to speak, or rather, my own body struggles to develop words to come out of my mouth.

Well, that doesn't help, but maybe the extra time to think will do me good, as I can't go forward with this man unless I know that I will never break his heart again.

CHAPTER TWENTY-ONE

JAKE

STANDING IN MY OVERSIZED RAIN SHOWER FULL OF steam, I let the hot water fall down my skin as I rub a hand through my hair and then take in the water on my face. As the hot water loosens my muscles, all I can do is hope that I got through to Avery. I didn't give her a chance to respond, and giving her time to think may or may not be good for me.

An exhale escapes me as my hand grips the shower faucet to turn off the water. Emerging out of the shower, I grab a towel that is waiting on the hanger next to the door. The steam clears as I take a few steps and I stop with a racing heart when I see who is in front of me.

"I told you not to give me your key," Avery states as she leans against the bathroom vanity, still in her black cotton dress from earlier.

Words cannot come out of my mouth, and she picks up on this.

"You left before I had a chance to speak," she continues.

Stepping closer to her, I study her face. Nothing. I get no indication. Nada.

"What would you have said?" I ask softly, and I can't help it, I let my hand find her hair.

A cheeky grin forms on her face. "That I figured you would have asked me to marry you then. It isn't a big shocker."

My face gives her a puzzled look. Have I gotten the magnitude of this all wrong?

"It's a no-brainer, Jake. You're an honorable guy, and you asking me to go away with you for a special trip when I was going to have your baby, well, the writing was on the wall. It's not a shocker, but hearing it now... it's the confirmation of what I always wondered. It's also a reminder of what didn't happen. I just needed some air to take it in."

"I wasn't going to ask because I was an honorable guy. I loved—I *love* you," I remind her. Her fingers run along my arm.

"I know. I know, because I loved you too." Her mouth hitches to the side.

Blood begins to rush at high speed in my veins.

"I love you now too, in case you were still wondering." An almost fun yet warm smile flashes to me as she says that.

"I'm scared," she begins. "I keep thinking you might change your mind or that you'll wake up one day with resentment that I walked away."

"I'm not letting you leave again."

She nods slowly. "I think I understand that now. We have nothing to hide, and we have our closure about what happened. You're right. We both made mistakes. But I am tired of letting guilt overcome me. I'm going to let it go. Look where we are now, Jake. A good place. Our road led us to a *good* life. I only want to try again and focus on the future." Her wry smile does not leave her. She tries to catch my eye. "You're in that future, in case you were wondering that too."

Our eyes hold, full of hope. "How do I look in your future?" I ask, stepping closer.

"Well, it's a long future," she tells me as my hand moves down her face.

"Yeah? What else?"

"You'll be in bed a lot... but not to sleep." Avery gives me a sexy smile.

My hand glides slowly through her silky hair. "Lucky me."

"My guess is I'll be lucky too. Since we will talk a lot, go for lots of walks, romantic dinners, try for a baby—"

"Lots of babies," I correct her as I begin to pull her head towards me.

She smiles. "Lots of babies. You'll never run away or let go. I'll never run away or let go. We will be really happy."

In record time, my lips find hers for a deep kiss, a melting kiss. Entirely greedy and so hard that it may just bruise her lips. Only when I pull away do I remind her, "I love you." My finger goes under her chin and I tip her head up for her eyes to look at me. My hands cup her face, and her hands hold my arms.

"We're okay, Jake," she murmurs.

She pulls away gently and looks at my left wrist, bringing it up to her lips, then letting a finger brush along my ring finger.

"The ring... ask me one day." It's a fact she states with the corner of her mouth forming a grin. "It's a nice ring you picked too."

"I will ask you one day. Soon. It will be right."

"I'd like that." Her smile grows.

My hands find the sides of her body and I guide her to

stand so her back is against my front. We're facing the mirror, looking at each other through the reflection.

"I'm yours. I only want to be yours," she tells me softly with purpose as our eyes meet in the glass.

Her look turns to lust and my face turns to an image of thirst.

My arms wrap around her as my mouth finds her neck with my lips placing a firm kiss on the place where her neck and shoulder meet.

Looking at each other in the mirror, we watch as I grab her hips and drag them back. Her arms straight ahead and hands firm on the sink. Quickly, I shimmy her dress above her waist and pull her underwear down to the floor that she steps out from. My towel disappears in a swift move.

My hands move to the top of her dress and bring the top halfway down as her perky breasts come free with hard red buds. Pressing into her back, my hands cup her breasts and tug her nipples as she lets out a moan. We continue to watch through the mirror.

Releasing a breast, my fingers slide down to her silky slit to check, and she feels eager. Grabbing my cock, I quickly find my way into her. Need spiraling below my navel, this is going to go fast and hard. There is a reason for this round, a point to prove. A confirmation to make.

Pushing hard into her, I find her depth before moving in and out.

Pulling her hair gently to bring her upper body up and pressed against my chest, I whisper into her ear as we watch. "Together. No other way. Together."

Her eyes have a sparkle of approval, and with that, I let her fall forward again. I lean forward so our fingers can interlace, as I press my body tightly against hers as I go deep and hard. It quickens and we're both letting moans, sighs, and cries escape us as we watch ourselves in the mirror.

Eventually, we both release and pant.

I stay in her as I fall to resting on her back and our fingers stay interlaced. After a moment, I pull out and she turns around, looping her arms around my neck and going up on her toes to kiss me deeply on the lips.

Sitting on the edge of the vanity, her legs wrap around my waist. Very easily, I could slip into her again. But instead, I just want to look into her eyes and say nothing.

After five minutes of staring at each other, stroking each other's cheeks with the occasional kiss on the lips, I carry her to bed where we spend the whole night entangled in each other.

CHAPTER TWENTY-TWO

"Great. Thanks, Avery," says the photographer as he looks at the shots on the back screen of his camera.

Stepping away from the display of cakes, I'm happy that it's finished, because an hour of photos of Smokey Java's, with me staged against trays of cakes, is enough to send me eating raw cookie dough from a bowl with a bottle of strong liquor in my other hand.

"You still need Tank?" Nate asks, as he is letting us borrow his dog for photos with baked dog treats.

"I don't know, maybe ask the photographer. Really appreciate this, Nate."

"No problem. My guy is a model," Nate says as he's on one knee and he rubs the dog's head.

"Do you mind if we do the interview now?" Dana the reporter asks. She seems like she's Jake's age, with dark hair and a sweater fit for a librarian.

I nod yes. "Of course."

Abby, who has been watching, quickly grabs my arm and pulls me to the side. "Come on, Avery. You got this. Just smile a little bit longer. I think it will be worth your while," she reassures me.

I give a nod of agreement and let my hand straighten my olive-green dress that is long and has straps, with sandals and accessories that honestly tip me to the edge of bohemian.

Adjusting my stance, I walk confidently to the table with the reporter, sitting down, and I offer her the tray of different baked goods.

"These are good," Dana remarks as she eats a chocolate chip cookie.

"Thanks."

"So, if you don't mind, I have some questions about the business and then a few personal questions, if that's okay?"

Business, fine, but unless the personal questions are about my preference of yoga or Pilates, then I am not a fan. But I will push through, it's for my business. So, I throw on my best professional smile.

After a few questions about re-inventing the menu with new recipes, moving from San Francisco and starting a dog treat line, Dana, who seems decent, switches the topic.

"I was wondering what you do in your spare time. Hobbies?"

Okay, that seems like a fair question, nothing too earth-shattering.

"I try and go to yoga classes and I started trail running since my boyfriend is a trail runner," I explain, and realize that I mentioned a boyfriend, and also that there is a big grin slapped across my face.

"Do you have a dog, since you also make dog treats?" Dana asks as she checks her phone is still recording.

I take a sip of my coffee. "No dog. We only have a goldfish," I shrug. It's our goldfish, because I moved into Jake's as soon as I could.

"We? Oh, so it's serious with your boyfriend?"

Whoa, now she's crossing the line into too personal. My warrior woman is coming out, yet I can't help the wide smile spreading across my face yet again. "Yeah, we are." It sends warmth and happiness through me.

Dana picks up on this and smiles. "Sounds like a good life. Okay, Avery, we're done. Thanks so much for doing this."

"No, thank *you*, and if you need anything else then let me know." I smile and show Dana out.

When Dana and her photographer are gone, I turn to Abby and Nate. "I need alcohol."

"Good thing I know a good bar," Nate grins.

"Come on, something tells me it'll be a good time," Abby smiles at Nate as she interlaces our arms.

We walk down the sidewalk to Matchbox, with Nate's dog Tank running ahead of us.

Arriving at Matchbox late on a weekday afternoon, it's not too busy. We head straight to the bar while Nate goes behind the counter to prepare us a drink. I lean against the bar to take a breath.

Abby starts to ponder. "Remember how Lucas and I tried to set you up with Jake, but you always said you weren't interested because his name is Jake? Something about been there, done that, etcetera."

"Yes, and?" I ask.

"So, there is a Jake we know, and we think you will like this Jake," Lucas says as he comes and drapes an arm around Abby. I study him. He's grinning a far-too-coy smile. Catching Abby beaming in the corner of my eye, I begin to realize that I should play along.

Shifting in my chair, I cross my arms and smile at Lucas. "Oh yeah? And why is that?"

"Pretty positive he isn't a stranger to you." Lucas grins.

"Oh yeah?" I challenge.

"Yeah. I would definitely say he's more than a stranger," he affirms again.

"In fact, he will probably be your husband," that all-too-familiar voice says from behind me.

My heart bounces in excitement, my stomach twirls like a merry-go-round, and my face is probably a mixture of a smile and tears forming. Turning around, I see my future in front of me.

There is Jake, who must have come straight from work, in his three-piece suit, on one knee with a bottle in hand, his charming smile on display.

"Hope you don't mind, I know you wanted me to wait with a bottle of wine after your interview, but I found this great bottle of mezcal," he states with delight in his voice.

My smile overtakes my face as I walk towards him slowly. When I reach him, I go to clutch his hand with the bottle that is the new Matchbox brand, which he did end up investing in. It's then that I notice there is a ring attached to the bottle by a little red string.

There is a pause as I look into his eyes.

"I would say there's no probably about it. You *will* be my husband." It comes out sentimental, as my gaze locks with his.

"So, you'll marry me?" he asks with a knowing grin.

I nod yes as tears floods my eyes. He gets up off his knee, his eyes never leaving me and my hand never leaving his.

"Yeah, yeah, I will." Before I can process anything else,

he pulls me into an embrace to kiss me deeply and passionately as he twirls me around.

Applause erupts from the people in the room. Abby and Lucas stand in a side hug as they watch us. Nate is by the door giving his dog a treat, with Leo's relative Melanie arriving behind him, and I wonder if the magic of Matchbox will send them down the same path as the rest of us. Jess, Leo, Max, and Harper are all clapping and must have been sitting at a table in the corner the whole time. Stella is jumping up and down, as Becca watches on with tears.

When I look back at Jake, we enter our own world again.

"You are sneaky."

"It's not too soon?" he asks.

I grab his wrist and slowly kiss his pulse next to his watch, letting my eyes look at him.

"No way. I have loved you for more than five years. And now that we got our again, I know. I know this is supposed to be," I remind him.

He grabs my wrist and kisses my pulse.

"I love you," he tells me.

"I really love you."

After pulling away from another kiss, I look at him with mischief in my eyes. "So, do you have some ideas of what to do with this bottle of mezcal?"

He gives me a smoldering look. "Many ideas, and something tells me our minds may have something in common," he warns, as our foreheads touch.

"Think we need to try that night with mezcal on the kitchen counter again," I urge.

He mutters something indescribable through his teeth and nibbles my ear, moving down to my neck.

"We will try many things," he warns with a devilish grin.

EPILOGUE

JAKE: A WHILE LATER

WRAPPING A TOWEL AROUND MY WAIST, HAVING JUST taken a shower after a long day in deposition for a client, I emerge into the bedroom. As soon as I see the sight in front of me, I know there was no point of having a towel, because this towel is only going to come off. My eyes roam my wife who is lying in the middle of the bed, waiting for me in lingerie that I picked out: a red satin dress that barely covers her.

Yet, I was not expecting this.

Avery gives me a seductive smile and lays her arms above her head on the bed.

"What are you doing?" I'm intrigued as I crawl on the bed on all fours, immediately coming to kiss her stomach and let my teeth capture the fabric between my teeth.

"Thought we could discuss a new merger," she teases.

"Ave," I warn.

In a quick movement, she pushes me to lying and straddles me.

"I got the all-clear. We can have crazy amounts of sex

again." She is dead serious as her mouth goes to my chest, covering me with little butterfly kisses.

"Yes, because our son will most definitely sleep normally so his parents can have a marathon of sex," I say sarcastically.

After getting married not long after I proposed, we decided to try for a baby. It went quick, and while we were both nervous at the start of the pregnancy, our anxiety eased the further along we went. We even did one of those labor and parenting courses with Jess and Leo, who were also expecting.

It has been six weeks since our little boy, Finn—named after my grandfather who passed away shortly before his namesake's birth—joined the world, and life has been changed.

"So, we will have to get creative. That's never been a problem for us."

"You are something, you know that?" I smile as I grab her and flip her, so she is lying on the bed underneath me.

"We will have to be fast all the time," she pouts.

"But more frequent?" I give her a challenging face.

"Whatever you say, just please, I need you in me," she begs as her legs wrap around me.

I'm not denying this woman a thing, not since she has made me the happiest man on earth.

I give it to her tenderly, as it's her first time since the birth. She moans into my mouth to try and not wake anyone in the house. Being quiet is a new criterion for our nights together. We sink into the middle of the bed, entangled in each other.

And we fall asleep.

...for a solid two hours before our son woke for a midnight feed.

The next morning, it's luckily Saturday. Not that it means much anymore, as either way our human alarm clock wakes at five A.M. But after going for a run, I return to a picture that makes the sleepless nights rewarding.

Avery has Finn in a wrap around her front as she cooks breakfast for us, the smell of fresh coffee filling our house. The little guy normally takes an early morning nap in the wrap, which means Avery and I can have an easy relaxed breakfast together, as she is on maternity leave and trained someone to handle the bakery while she's off.

I kiss her cheek as she puts toast on a plate.

"Hmm, you're sweaty," she says as she walks to the other side of the kitchen island.

"Yeah, I'll shower after breakfast. Lunch with everyone is at 1, right?" I mention as I pour myself some coffee.

"Maybe if our son cooperates, then I can lay him in his bed and join you in the shower." She cocks a brow my way.

"I like your thinking," I confirm with a grin.

"Yeah, lunch is at 1, at Max and Harper's house. I'm kind of hoping Max had his mom cook some food. Harper's cooking is a little shaky at times." Avery has a cartoonish face and I love her honesty.

"It's okay, you're bringing dessert, so least we know we're all safe with that."

Sitting next to her on a stool at the counter, I grab a piece of toast. My phone vibrates on the counter, and I quickly glance to see a text message from my sister that makes me laugh before I type back.

"Be nice," Avery warns me with glaring eyes.

"What? After years of her hounding me in my romantic life, I can repay her in full as she re-enters the dating world." I move my phone away and look at Avery. I admire the view of her looking down at our son with a radiant smile and soft eyes. Her hand with our wedding ring on it holding Finn's head who is sleeping peacefully.

"You look really happy today," I reflect.

She leans to the side as I wrap an arm around her and she buries her head into my chest. "I am. We finally get to have fun in the bedroom again. I have a husband, and we made a beautiful baby boy. How are you feeling today?"

I kiss her forehead. "Pretty damn good. We got our again, and we ended up where we were always meant to be."

Her mouth hitches up as she grabs my wrist with my watch, bringing my inner pulse to her mouth for a soft tender kiss.

"It's never going to change again," she reminds me.

My only response is the best kind. My mouth firmly planting on her lips for a kiss.

THANK YOU

Anyone who read this book, I can't tell you how much it means to me. Whether you're new to the Matchbox series or you are following all the characters, I hope you enjoyed.

Lindsay from Contagious Edits, ah, magic you are! Thanks so much for everything. Especially as every Matchbox book is well... different.

Katy from Once Upon a Proofread, thanks for taking on the task of being an extra set of eyes.

My close friend and fellow toddler-date chaperone, thanks for beta-reading during a crazy time.

Thanks to my offspring and my version of Prince Charming, always hanging in there while I live off of writing, coffee, and whiskey (not even in that order).

Made in United States
North Haven, CT
04 January 2023

30596948R00124